D.   . C

(Immortal Outcasts)

by

Mandy M. Roth

Suggested reading order of books
released to date in the
***Immortal Ops Series* world**

Immortal Ops

Critical Intelligence

Radar Deception

Strategic Vulnerability

Tactical Magik

Act of Mercy

Administrative Control

Act of Surrender

Broken Communication

Separation Zone

Act of Submission

Damage Report

More to come (check www.mandyroth.com
for new releases)

Mandy M. Roth, Online

Mandy loves hearing from readers and can be found interacting on social media.

(copy & paste links into your browser window)

Website: http://www.MandyRoth.com

Blog: http://www.MandyRoth.com/blog

The Raven Books: http://www.TheRavenBooks.com

Facebook: http://www.facebook.com/AuthorMandyRoth

Twitter: @MandyMRoth

Book Release Newsletter: mandyroth.com/newsletter.htm

(Newsletters: I do not share emails and only send newsletters when there is a new release/contest/or sales)

Mandy M. Roth Featured Books

Immortal Ops Series

Immortal Ops
Critical Intelligence
Radar Deception
Strategic Vulnerability
Tactical Magik
Administrative Control
Separation Zone
Area of Influence
Desired Perception
Carnal Diversions
Zone of Action

PSI-Ops Series (Part of the Immortal Ops World)

Act of Mercy
Act of Surrender
Act of Submission
Act of Security
Act of Command
Act of Passion
Act of Engagement
Act of Pride
Act of Duty

Immortal Outcasts (Part of the Immortal Ops World)

Broken Communication
Damage Report

Damage Report

- Wrecked Intel
- Isolated Maneuver
- Intelligence Malfunction

Shadow Agents Series & Crimson Sentinels Series (Part of the Immortal Ops World) Coming Soon!

Praise for Mandy M. Roth's Immortal Ops World

Silver Star Award—*I feel Immortal Ops deserves a Silver Star Award as this book was so flawlessly written with elements of intrigue, suspense and some scorching hot scenes*—Aggie Tsirikas—Just Erotic Romance Reviews

5 Stars—*Immortal Ops is a fascinating short story. The characters just seem to jump out at you. Ms. Roth wrote the main and secondary characters with such depth of emotions and heartfelt compassion I found myself really caring for them*—Susan Holly—Just Erotic Romance Reviews

Immortal Ops packs the action of a Hollywood thriller with the smoldering heat that readers can expect from Ms. Roth. Put it on your hot list...and keep it there! —The Road to Romance

5 Stars—*Her characters are so realistic, I find myself wondering about the fine line between fact and fiction...This was one captivating tale that I did not want to end. Just the right touch of humor*

endeared these characters to me even more — eCataRomance Reviews

5 Steamy Cups of Coffee — *Combining the world of secret government operations with mythical creatures as if they were an everyday thing, she (Ms. Roth) then has the audacity to make you actually believe it and wonder if there could be some truth to it. I know I did. Nora Roberts once told me that there are some people who are good writers and some who are good storytellers, but the best is a combination of both and I believe Ms. Roth is just that. Mandy Roth never fails to surpass herself* — coffeetimeromance

Mandy Roth kicks ass in this story — inthelibraryreview

Immortal Ops Series and PSI-Ops Series Helper

(This will be updated in each upcoming book as new characters are introduced.)

Immortal Ops (I-Ops) Team Members

Lukian Vlakhusha: Alpha-Dog-One. Team captain, werewolf, King of the Lycans, mated to Peren Matthews (Daughter of Dr. Lakeland Matthews). Book: Immortal Ops (Immortal Ops)

Geoffroi (Roi) Majors: Alpha-Dog-Two. Second-in-command, werewolf, blood-bound brother to Lukian, mated to Melissa "Missy" Carter-Majors. Book: Critical Intelligence

(Immortal Ops)

Doctor Thaddeus Green: Bravo-Dog-One. Scientist, tech guru, werepanther, mated to Melanie Daly-Green (sister of Eadan Green). Book: Radar Deception (Immortal Ops)

Jonathon (Jon) Reynell: Bravo-Dog-Two. Sniper, weretiger, mated to Tori Manzo. Book: Separation Zone (Immortal Ops)

Wilson Rousseau: Bravo-Dog-Three. Resident smart-ass, wererat, mated to Kimberly (Daughter of Culann of the Council) Book: Strategic Vulnerability (Immortal Ops)

Eadan Daly: Alpha-Dog-Three. PSI-Op and handler on loan to the I-Ops to round out the team, Fae, mated to Inara Nash. Brother of Melanie Daly-Green. Book: Tactical Magik (Immortal Ops)

Colonel Asher Brooks: Chief of Operations and point person for the Immortal Ops Team. Mated to Jinx, magik, succubus, well-known, well-connected madam to the underground paranormal community. Book: Administrative Control (Immortal Ops)

Paranormal Security and Intelligence

(PSI) Operatives

General Jack C. Newman: Director of Operations for PSI North American Division, werelion. Adoptive father of Missy Carter-Majors.

Duke Marlow: PSI-Operative, werewolf. Mated to Mercy. Book: Act of Mercy (PSI-Ops)

Doctor James (Jimmy) Hagen: PSI-Operative, werewolf. Took a ten-year hiatus from PSI. Mated to Laney. Book: Act of Surrender (PSI-Ops)

Striker (Dougal) McCracken: PSI-Operative, werewolf.

Miles (Boomer) Walsh: PSI-Operative, werepanther. Mated to Haven. Book: Act of Submission (PSI-Ops)

Captain Corbin Jones: Operations coordinator and captain for PSI-Ops Team Five, werelion.

Malik (Tut) Nasser: PSI-Operative, (PSI-Ops).

Colonel Ulric Lovett: Director of Operations, PSI-London Division.

Immortal Outcasts

Casey Black: I-Ops test subject, werewolf, mated to Harmony. Book: Broken Communication.

Weston Carol: I-Ops test subject, were-bear.

Bane Antonov: I-Ops test subject, were-gorilla.

Miscellaneous

Culann of the Council: Father to Kimberly (who is mated to Wilson). Badass Fae.

Pierre Molyneux: Master vampire bent on creating a race of super soldiers. Hides behind being a famous art dealer in order to launder money.

Gisbert Krauss: Mad scientist who wants to create a master race of supernaturals.

Walter Helmuth: Head of Seattle's paranormal underground. In league with Molyneux and Krauss.

Dr. Lakeland Matthews: Scientist, vital role in the creation of a successful Immortal

Ops Team. Father to Peren Matthews.

Dr. Bertrand: Mad scientist with Donavon Dynamics Corporation (The Corporation).

Damage Report
Book Two in the Immortal Outcasts Series

New York Times and USA Today
Bestselling Series the Immortal Outcasts!
Part of the Immortal Ops World!

Weston Carol—bear-shifter, genetically
altered super soldier—just wants to return
to his solitary life off the grid. As far as
he's concerned, after helping to rescue the
mate of his former teammate, he's done
his good deed for the decade. Now he
simply wants to retreat to the woods
where he can drop off the radar of those
looking to kill him.

Then news reaches him of a woman in
danger and he can't help but rescue the
damsel in distress. Whether or not he
believes it, she is his future, and he's in
no condition to meet his mate. It's been
too long since he's seen to his manly
needs, and way too long without shifting—
he's a tense, grumpy mess on the verge of

losing control of his bear side. One small stop on the way shouldn't interfere with fate too much, right?

Chapter One

If Weston Carol didn't shift into a bear soon, he was going to tear someone's head off and possibly munch on their skull like a jawbreaker. He didn't much care that he'd be picking bone bits out of his teeth for weeks. Wouldn't be the first time. And it sure as hell wouldn't be the last. His life had been long and hard. There were things in his past he wasn't proud of and things in his future he was sure to come to regret.

Such was the way of it all.

He was tired, in need of a shift, hungry, and he wanted sex. He wasn't even sure in what order he needed it to happen, only that it all needed to happen sooner rather than later. The shifting was winning out. Though, he'd have put money on his dick needing satisfied first and foremost. Guess the bear in him had other plans.

His bear was an asshole.

Add in the fact he was exhausted and hadn't slept worth a damn for weeks because of screwed-up dreams, and Weston was pretty much a raging bear waiting to happen. He rubbed his jaw, his hands moving over his closely clipped beard. He'd never been one of those clean-shaven kind of guys. Wasn't his thing. Even before becoming a shifter.

A lot had changed after his testing. His grooming habits weren't one of them. Neither were the dreams. He'd had those for as long as he could remember, but whatever had been done to him years ago had made them much more intense.

Intense.

Telling.

Sometimes horrifying.

Closing his eyes for a moment, he relaxed and thought about one of the dreams that had been both soothing and oddly terrifying. The one with the faceless woman. He could see her from behind, her long hair down and going in all directions, curly and glorious—made for a man to run his fingers through. And he could smell her.

Berries and cream.

The scent was burned into his brain. He wanted to wrap himself in it. His mouth watered with desire as he opened his eyes, his attention now on the woods before him. He couldn't keep dwelling on whatever it was his dreams were trying to tell him. He'd already listened to his fucked-up dreams once in the month and had come out of hiding to do so. He'd spent decades staying under the radar of people who wanted to study him or kill him, and he'd flushed it all to help a friend. Someone he considered a brother.

Weston had sought out Casey Black, a fellow Immortal Outcast, and even assisted the guy's mate. When Weston's dreams had led him to believe that Casey's mate, Harmony, would be taken captive and killed, he found he couldn't stay hidden any longer. He had to do something to try to stop the events from unfolding. He had. Sort of. When it was over, she'd been alive and unharmed, but he'd been a bit late to the party, so to speak, and she'd been taken captive. That had left him no choice but to get himself captured as well—to be sure he was taken straight to her, as he had been. He'd been drugged, chained and imprisoned—again.

Though not for long.

Since he'd allowed himself to be captured in the first place, he'd always been in control of the situation, at least to some degree. And he had to laugh at the men who had tried to keep him held prisoner. What jokes. They were the type who probably had trouble catching and keeping a bug in a jar when they were little.

Idiots.

Dead idiots now, but idiots all the same.

No, Weston had done his due diligence. He'd helped another Outcast. Paid some good forward. Now, though, his work was done and he didn't need to stay in the area any longer. With Harmony home safe, the dreams should have eased up or at least stopped for a while. In the past, once the danger was over, he'd always been given breaks.

Not now. The Harmony dreams ended only for new, more confusing ones to begin, and they'd started when Weston was drugged and held captive. Whatever sedative they'd pumped him full of was more than likely a trigger. Though, he didn't understand how or why.

The dreams brought with them the sinking feeling something bad was close to happening to someone he loved. But since he didn't love anyone that in itself was confusing. So was the berries-and-cream girl. He'd never been blocked from being able to see a face in his dreams before, but hers was a mask of nothingness to him. Whoever she was, he had a strong sense that she was either in trouble or about to be, but he didn't have any details beyond that. Didn't matter how many times he tried to dream of her, all the information he received from whatever it was he tapped into when he was asleep wasn't much to go on.

"Some gift you assholes gave me. Should have kept my receipt and demanded a refund," he ground out between clenched teeth, thinking of the scientists who made him what he was today. They'd messed up with him and others like him.

Big time.

And there wasn't anyone to complain to. No one to rat them out to. The people who'd done this to him didn't exist on paper. They were ghosts. Men like them had been around forever and a day, getting away with atrocities all in the name of science. Several of the scientists in the Ops program when it started were true monsters in every sense of the word. Over the decades, new ones were brought in. Ones who had visions of an end goal but weren't willing to kill to get to it. Weston understood that everyone involved in the program wasn't evil to the core. And despite all he'd been put through, he understood the need for men like him— soldiers who could shift into animals or something more. That didn't lessen the sting of it all any or take away from the horrors he'd endured.

The endless tests. The painful operations. The poking, the prodding and, in the end, what could only be labeled as torture before they outright tried to kill him.

It all took its toll on him.

Left him wanting to curl away from society and simply exist alone. After escaping their clutches, he began learning about the history of similar programs. It was amazing how much was documented in books and old journals. How much was there for the public to view and yet very few did. And when he'd reached out to contacts in the underground, he found even more information.

It was scary as hell to see just how many times comparable tests were done, some even known worldwide, like Ilya Ivanov and his ape-army attempts. Ivanov had been one of Hitler's scientists, and he and so many others had participated in what would be later called Nazi's Eugenics and the attempts at creating a master race. The Nazis weren't the only offenders. Weston was living proof of just how caught up in it all America had been, and in truth probably still was.

He didn't believe for one second they'd stopped their programs to create super soldiers. They'd just gotten better at hiding it. Other countries kept their attempts out of the papers and out of sight of humans, but supernaturals knew the truth. Knew the programs and tests were out there. Knew people were still trying to play God and that they were failing in unimaginable ways.

Gisbert Krauss was just one of the masterminds behind some of the new creations, such as the hybrids Weston had come up against more than once in the past year. From what he'd been told, many of the hybrids had started off as full-blooded supernaturals, and after Krauss and his team of scientists were done with them they were officially monsters. Blends of so many things, some of them no longer resembled human.

Weston shivered.

No thanks.

Sharing himself with a bear was bad enough. His skin burned with the need for a change, and since he was currently alone, sex would have to wait. Yanking on himself was never his favorite way to get off. He preferred a hot chick to his hand, but had been known to resort to his hand when nothing else would do. Such would be the case soon enough at the rate he was going.

He'd been unable to roam free in bear form for weeks and he couldn't take one more day of it. He pulled his truck off to the side of the road near a large expanse of black walnut trees and a deep-set ravine and got out, his entire body tense. He couldn't tell if he wanted to shift forms or just go on a killing spree. At the moment, both were in a dead heat. Never a good sign when you were doing your best to walk the path of the righteous.

He nearly laughed at the idea he was holier than thou.

Hardly.

He had been to church in his lifetime, more than once even, but that was before he'd become what he was. Before the military and government scientists tried to play God. Before he ended up sharing his body with an ill-tempered bear who, when he didn't get his way, got downright deadly. Though in all fairness, he'd apparently been hiding the genes needed to shift shapes somewhere deep in his genetic makeup, which was why he was a success when so many others were a failure. But the scientists couldn't stop there. They couldn't be content. No, they had wanted even more. Even better. They'd made him something even supernaturals were timid around.

A shapeshifter with the power of a bear, a wolf, and a tiger all wrapped in one. He couldn't shift into a wolf or tiger, but he carried trace amounts of their DNA. That wasn't all. He had other abilities. Ones he'd been born with that the scientists had wanted to enhance to serve their own purposes. Didn't work out as planned, though. He didn't end up a savior to the world or even his country. Hell, he didn't even end up something they could use. He'd been cast aside, and then they'd tried to eliminate him. Apparently, they couldn't have an unpredictable bear-shifter running about. Especially one with the gift of foresight.

He'd done well at keeping his head down and simply existing. He'd managed to turn a decent profit, taking money for hire jobs that utilized his skill set. Most of the jobs were for unsavory folks, doing illegal things, but the money was green and spent the same. Plus, no one asked for paperwork or made him fill out government forms. They just let him do his job and leave. No muss. No fuss.

Perfect.

"I'm a gun for hire," he said softly with a slight snort, hating saying it out loud. He'd only ever wanted to do good with his life, but circumstances hadn't allowed for that. Though, for every bad job he took, Weston tried to balance it out with an act of kindness. Like giving all the proceeds from certain jobs to charities. He wasn't all bad. At least not yet.

He was a guy who'd spent the last few decades trying to make amends for being a piece of shit earlier in life. So far, he wasn't close to even. Didn't help that he, like many of the surviving Outcasts, hired out for mercenary-like jobs, taking work where they could get it while living off the grid. It wasn't a glamorous life, but the pay was good and it kept him out of the clutches of a government that would rather see him dead than admit they screwed up.

And *boy,* did they screw up.

He tugged at the bottom of his t-shirt. He'd bought the shirt, with a photo of a favorite rock band on the front of it, during a concert back in the seventies, and the piece of crap "vintage" ones retailers tried to pawn off on hipsters in the current market didn't compare, so Weston took the time to remove it— shifting forms in it would leave it in shreds.

He kicked his boots off and went to work on the button to his jeans. He couldn't seem to get out of his clothes fast enough. Dammit. His body burned with the need to change. To let the bear in him run and then wander the woods, doing whatever the fuck it was bears liked to do. He never understood the lure of half of what his bear side found fun. Picking berries in human form didn't do jack crap for him, but apparently, his bear side enjoyed it immensely. Weston just knew if he didn't get it together and shift soon, the bear would more than likely go on a homicidal rampage.

Weston, like his bear, wasn't anything anyone would ever label as scrawny. Standing well over six feet, he had the mass to match his height and kept his bulk to just this side of being too much. He'd met men in the past who were all about trying to be the biggest and baddest. Most often they ended up being the slowest. Weston liked a mix of speed and strength. And there wasn't much he could do about his height. He'd been born with it. Normally, that wasn't too much of an issue, unless he was entering a room with low doorways. But as he tried to shimmy out of his clothing, he found his size a hindrance. He hopped on one foot as he tugged off his jeans. The moment he was fully naked and about to shift forms, headlights pierced the darkness on the road that was rarely traveled.

"Son of a bitch," he shouted, stepping behind the side of his truck, knowing he'd already been seen in all his naked glory. He had no issue with nudity, but humans tended to. They were prudish, to say the least. He didn't need the local sheriff showing up to question him about his midnight escapades.

The SUV pulled to a stop in front of his truck and Weston groaned when the driver stepped out. It wasn't the sheriff, but that wasn't saying much. He stared at his fellow Outcast and friend. "Casey, are you stalking me? Man, if you wanted to see me naked you just had to ask. You didn't need to hunt me down."

"Heard you'd be here." The tall, raven-haired man flipped Weston off and then opened the back door to his SUV. When a tiny, wiry-haired man who looked a lot like he belonged in a mental ward exited the SUV and was then followed by a thin, pale man who stared in any direction but at a person, Weston tipped his head. The two sidekicks seemed to be attached to Casey of late. One was goofier than the other.

"You brought them here? Why?" he

demanded, naked and unconcerned.

Casey pinched the bridge of his nose. They'd been friends a long time. The stress in Casey's expression warned Weston there was more to this than he was going to like. Casey pointed to the thin, pale guy. "Gus insisted we come."

"He's the mind reader, right?" asked Weston, stepping out from behind his truck and crossing his arms over his chest. He didn't give a rat's ass that his junk was there for everyone to see. Let them look.

Whatever.

The wiry-haired guy's gaze snapped right to Weston's package. "Wow. The scientists gave you that?"

Weston's gums burned with the need to change and eat the tiny nuisance. "Casey."

Casey touched the small man's shoulders. "Bill, remember what we talked about on the way over?"

Bill nodded. "Stand still. Don't talk. If I don't listen, the bear guy might eat me."

"That's right," said Casey, sounding

more like a primary school teacher trying to soothe a small child than the bad-ass super soldier he was. "So asking Weston about his dick counts as talking."

Bill touched his chin and did an obvious ponder over Casey's statement. He shrugged and looked around Casey, pointing to Weston's groin. "Did you get a look at that? Are you all hung like that? Where do I sign up for that test and enhancement? All I got was LSD. Who do I complain to? We should get those standard at the door if we get tested on by the government. Seems the least they could do."

Weston tipped his head. "Can I eat him, please?"

Casey glanced over his shoulder. "He really can't help himself. They did a number on him."

"They did a number on us all, but you don't see me asking about his dick," stated Weston. No sooner did the words leave his mouth than the crazy little guy started to remove his clothing. The guy was furrier than Weston was in shifted form. And the man had nothing Weston wanted to see. "Seriously, I'm going to eat him. It would be a service to mankind."

Casey grabbed the crazy man. "Bill, no getting naked. We've already had this talk."

Gus began to pace back and forth, flapping one of his hands in the air as he did. "More than once. Had the talk more than once."

Casey glanced in the pale's guy direction. "Gus, no need to get worked up. I've got this. Go stand by Weston's truck."

"Great, I get the nut job who is tuned in to channel static," muttered Weston, only partially under his breath. He still couldn't figure out why Casey saddled himself with these two. They were dead weight. They weren't shifters. They weren't part of the Immortal Ops testing, where the government had tried to make super soldiers, like Casey and Weston had been. No. Gus and Bill were humans who had gotten caught up in government testing—

the not-too-fucked-up stuff and honestly that wasn't saying much when you had men who could shift into animal as a comparison.

"He's naked. I wanna be naked too," argued Bill, sounding childlike rather than the old man he was. "All the rage, apparently."

"Had the talk more than once," continued Gus, sounding like a broken record. He turned in fast circles near Weston, making Weston slightly dizzy. "More than once."

Weston groaned and snatched his jeans from the ground. He wasn't going to get to wander and run tonight. Damn Casey for being a bleeding heart. The guy had always been that way. Hell, he'd befriended Weston because of it when many others wouldn't have dared to get near him. "Want to tell me why you're here? And why it is you brought the two stooges with you."

Casey had hold of Bill's pants and was trying to keep them on the wiry little man.

"Shit. Bill, come on. Cut me a break here."

Gus paced more and then pounded on the hood of Weston's truck. "Got to warn him. Got to warn him."

"This one sprung a brain leak," said Weston to Casey. "If he gets any brain goo on my truck, I'm gonna eat him. That crap is hard to wash off."

Gus stopped pacing and turned, his attention near Weston, and that meant something. The guy normally didn't appear to pay full attention to anything. The hair on the back of Weston's neck rose a second before he heard the man in his mind—on the same mental path the I-Ops had been trained to use. *She's in danger.*

Weston's gaze whipped to Casey. *You hear him in your head too?*

I do, returned Casey on the same mental path.

Gus wasn't a shifter and he wasn't an Immortal Op or even one of the failed Op attempts—an Outcast. He was something entirely different, and the guy had somehow managed to tap into their mental path of communication. Whatever he was, something deep in Weston's gut gnawed at him, demanding he at least hear the nut job out before dismissing him.

"Who is in danger? Harmony?" he asked. He wasn't sure why Casey would come running to *him* if his mate was in danger, but not a lot had been making sense lately. From the moment Weston had surfaced, letting others know he wasn't dead, things had been plain old weird. He was pissed he hadn't just stayed hidden. Things were simpler then. None of this drama bullshit.

He sighed, knowing that had he remained hidden, Casey's mate would have died. When Weston had learned Casey had a mate and that she was in danger, he'd stopped hiding in the shadows and he'd gone on a mission in search of the young woman. Harmony was feisty, opinionated, spoiled and someone he considered a friend. And he didn't have too many of those. "She okay?"

Casey held Bill off the ground by his

belt. "Harmony is safe at home. Laney is over with her and James is hovering. They're trying to shut down sites that are posting information about the Ops testing. And they're also trying to assist in finding any sort of a digital trail to Lance."

"The I-Op guy?" asked Weston. "So rumors are true? He's not six feet under?"

Casey shook his head. "Nope. More like six shades in the wind. He's a puppet for an asshole vampire who is working with the regular known bad guys."

"Krauss and Helmuth?" asked Weston, his interest piqued. He'd been looking into each of them for some time. One was worse than the other and they'd taken to teaming up. Never a good sign.

Casey nodded. "And some vampire."

"Shit. And you're sure Harmony and Laney are safe?"

"Yep. James is with them. Why?" asked Casey, still struggling with Bill.

Weston thumbed at Gus who was now batting at the air around his head as if bugs were bothering him. "He jacked my brain and said she's in danger. I thought he meant Harmony."

Casey sighed. "James is with the girls. They're fine."

Weston snorted. Of course James was near them. The guy was mated to Laney, Harmony's best friend. Made sense. Casey wouldn't go far from Harmony if she didn't have a protector nearby. James would do.

Weston eyed Gus who was now spinning in a circle. "Is his head gonna pop off?"

Casey carried Bill over and gave Weston a pleading look. "Can you get dressed so he stops trying to get naked?"

"Free Willy!" yelled the crazed man. He jerked around in Casey's arms, attempting to break free. "Let me be free! I want to feel the wind on my face."

"It's not your face you want wind on," said Casey, struggling to keep Bill clothed.

Weston slipped his jeans back on and put his arms out wide. "See. Covered."

Bill stopped acting a fool and calmed in Casey's arms. "You let the man win. I've lost all respect for you, Yogi."

"Yogi?" he asked.

Casey paled. "As in the bear."

Weston nearly laughed. For a crazy guy, he was amusing. "Casey, let the guy run naked in the woods. What harm can he do?"

Casey's eyes widened. "If you only knew."

Bill beamed. "You're all right by me, Yogi."

"Call me that again and I will break you in two," warned Weston. He was touchy about his bear-shifter side.

Bill pursed his lips. "Can I call you Papa Bear?"

Weston stared at Casey. "Really, it would be nothing for me to kill him and take him off your hands."

Casey snorted. "I'll think about it. Now, Weston, please listen. Gus insisted we track you down."

Weston watched Gus as he swatted at nothing. He lifted a brow, wondering why the hell the crazy guy would want to find him. And how he'd managed to find him so quickly. Instead of asking, he looked to Casey, waiting for his friend to explain it all.

Casey grabbed Bill by the belt loop and faced Weston. "I trust Gus. He's different but he's brilliant, and he's connected to stuff we can't begin to understand."

"Okay," said Weston, waiting for the point.

"He says your mate is in trouble," stated Casey, sucking in a large breath afterwards.

Weston snorted, trying to play off the concern that lanced through him. His most recent dreams came flooding back to him, and for a split second he even smelled berries and cream. Weston fought to stay in control as he looked to Gus. He'd heard of what Gus could do, of the man's special gifts, but Weston wasn't sure he was totally ready to believe in them. Didn't matter that he possessed enough of his own to make people doubt him too at times. He wanted to know everything the strange guy knew, but it wasn't like him to ask for help. He'd been on his own for far too long to start now. "I don't have a mate."

"Said just about every alpha male until he happens upon his," countered Casey snidely. He then stepped forward, yanking Bill with him. "You saved my mate. I'm here to try to return that favor. If Gus says she's in trouble, I believe him. So should you."

Weston held his sharp-witted response and went with, "Okay, does he have any idea who this mate of mine is? That would be the first step to this, right? Before we can save her, don't we have to know who she is?"

Casey glanced at Gus. "He told me you needed to go to Seattle. That you'd cross paths with her there and that you needed to go soon."

"And you buy into this all?" asked Weston, already knowing his friend did. They'd both seen too much in their lives to discount anything, no matter how weird it seemed. "You think I should drop everything and head cross-country to a huge city, and I'll just magically walk into my supposed mate? A mate I don't think exists."

Berries and cream, said Gus in Weston's mind, making him gasp and nearly lose his composure. *She smells like berries and cream.*

Casey let go of Bill but gave him a stern look.

Bill grinned. "I win."

"If Gus isn't wrong?" asked Casey, ignoring the small man's goading.

Weston's gut tensed. "I'm listening to him. I'll head to Seattle and see what I can scare up information-wise there. I appreciate the heads up."

"You want me to head to Seattle with you?" asked Casey. "We might have better luck if two of us are looking."

Shaking his head, Weston reached for his shirt. "No, man, you've got a brand new bride here, and with the shit that's been going down, it would be unwise to travel that far from her."

The look on Casey's face said he knew as much. "But I will, for you."

"I know. But no. I'll go alone."

Bill clapped. "Gus and I will go with you!"

Weston's expression sank. He was not signing on to babysit anyone. "Hell no."

Casey's lips pursed. "You know, that may work. Bill speaks fluent Gus and Gus is somehow tapping into your mate and her destiny."

"Is this a trick to get me to take the stooges from you?" Weston pulled his shirt over his head. "You realize you'll never see them again because I'll eat them."

Bill moved closer to Casey. "Tell him I don't taste good without hot sauce."

"Tell him I can hear him," returned Weston, snapping his jaws at the man.

Bill jumped in place.

Gus paused in his circles and looked something close to the direction Weston was standing in. "We'll pack."

"Oh, no," said Weston, shaking his

head. "No!"

Chapter Two

"How was the plane ride?" asked Casey, a teasing note in his voice.

Weston had to keep from crushing his cell phone with one hand as he held it to his ear and glanced over to be sure his traveling companions weren't getting into any more trouble. "Eat me, dickhead. You know exactly how the plane ride was."

Casey laughed. "Forgot to tell you that Gus doesn't fly well."

"Yeah, I figured that out at the thirty thousand feet mark," said Weston, harshly. He cracked his knuckles, wanting very much to hit Casey. In fact, the next time he laid eyes on the prick he'd show him just how great the plane ride had been. Had Weston known exactly what he'd been signing up for when he'd agreed to take the two stooges with him, he'd have driven cross-country. Instead, he'd had to hogtie a man mid-flight and nearly shackle the other as well. Probably why Casey neglected to mention Gus's flying skills, or lack thereof.

"Is Gus still breathing?" asked Casey, concern in his voice.

"By sheer luck, brother," returned Weston, the tension in his body keeping the bear in him on edge. The bear wasn't much on flying, either. Went against the natural order of things. "And you forgot to tell me how much Bill loves to fly. And I fucking mean he loves it."

"Oh no," breathed Casey, following it with a clicking of his tongue. "Dare I ask?"

Weston sighed, feeling like he'd just spent the last few hours herding cats. Hell, cats would have been easier. In truth, he'd simply been trying to keep Gus and Bill from bringing down the private plane they'd been on. One screamed like a bloody fool and the other was simply insane. "You're damn lucky the guy I chartered the flight with owed me. Bill would have gotten us arrested if we'd dared to fly commercial. He demanded he be allowed to help pilot the thing, and then wanted us all to make a break for it. To fly to the sun. To get out before the man and his brainwashed minions could try to stop us. Then he thought for sure he saw the President of the United States sitting on our right wing, winking at him. I think he may have been tripping."

"I forgot to check him for LSD before you left," said Casey. "Sorry. Harmony wasn't happy when she realized I let them go off with you all alone. Laney is pissed with me too. She seems to think you'll eat them both."

"I might." He'd considered it more than once. Though they were starting to grow on him, not that he'd tell Casey.

"Weston, it would be a big favor to me if

you didn't," said Casey. "They're kind of like family at this point."

"I know. Which is why they're both still alive." Weston glanced over to see Bill chatting it up with another pilot. "Listen, I gotta go. Bill is now trying to talk himself onto a large jetliner. Shit, I think he's offering the guy weed. Where is he hiding all the drugs?"

"You may want to do an anal cavity search," said Casey with a laugh that stopped quickly. "And, no, I'm not kidding."

"Asshole." He hung up and rushed over in Bill's direction. The man had on an old-fashioned flight cap and huge goggles. He'd arrived at the airport before they left wearing them. No amount of pleading had gotten him out of them. Weston just hoped he didn't keep them on for good.

Bill put his arms out wide and began to run around the tarmac near another pilot. Much to the other pilot's credit, he didn't comment on Bill's antics. Gus stood perfectly still as Bill made loops around him. Bill stopped and stared at his buddy. He then glanced over at Weston. "Gus is mad at you for making him fly. He wanted a window seat."

Pinching the bridge of his nose, Weston did his best to avoid losing his temper and shifting right there for all to see. Gus and Bill were going to make him a master of self-control by the end of the journey. He was sure of it. That, or he'd really eat them. Either was possible.

He grabbed Bill, pulling him closer to him and away from the other pilot. The man tipped his hat. "Interesting friends you have there."

Weston pressed a smile to his face and nodded. "They're something all right. Sorry if they bothered you. We'll be on our way now."

"Can I drive?" Bill shoved something into Weston's front jacket pocket. "Here. You hide these in case the feds show up."

Groaning, Weston pulled another bag of weed from Bill's jacket and growled as he grabbed Gus with the same hand he had the bag of pot in. "Come on."

Gus started to yell and swat at Weston.

Bill shook his head. "He doesn't like being touched."

"Would he rather be tied up and gagged?" Weston had very little patience for Gus's behavior.

Bill's expression grew somber. "You're mean, like the black-eyed one. The meanie mc-meanie."

Weston had heard Bill calling Duke Marlow, a Paranormal Security and Intelligence Agent, the name more than once. "Yeah, I make Duke look like a fucking ball of sunshine. Now let's go."

"Fine, but I'll get Gus. Not you, Grumpy Bear." Bill stopped and put his thumbs in his ears and waved his hands, sticking out his tongue as he did. "Grumpy Bear. Grumpy Bear."

"I'm going to flush your goods," warned Weston.

Bill snapped his mouth shut and reached for Gus. "Come on, Gus. We have to be nice so I can get the good shit back.

You understand, right?"

Weston continued to growl as he followed behind the two. He had to stop and grab their bags, though he did consider leaving them. Bill probably only packed drugs anyway. Weston spotted another of his contacts as they stepped out of a SUV near the side of a small hanger. It had been years since he'd last seen Bane Antonov. They'd spoken on the phone and had sent cryptic messages back and forth for the last few decades, but Weston hadn't had eyes on Bane since before they all broke out of the secret government holding facility.

Bane's black hair was long now. Much longer than Weston remembered it being. Gone was the high and tight they'd both sported for a time when they served together. Their baby faces were a thing of the past too. Bane had a decent amount of facial hair, something else he'd not had last time they'd seen one another. Emotions Weston didn't want to focus on surfaced. This was a man who had shared a similar experience with him. As had Casey. They knew what it was like to be chosen. To be told you were special, fall for lies and empty promises, and then be discarded like trash when things didn't go as planned. They knew what it was like to be hunted by the very people who made the empty promises. The people they'd dedicated their lives to, entrusting they would be made into assets for their country. Not ticking time-bombs.

They were Outcasts. Men who weren't considered stable investments. Men who were flawed somehow in the eyes of their creators. And Weston was certainly flawed.

Weston grunted at Bill as the man glanced back at him. Bill kept Gus walking forward, in Bane's direction. As they grew nearer, Bane glanced down from what looked like an imposing height when compared to Bill and Gus, though he was at eye level with Weston. "They don't look very elite."

Weston snorted, missing Bane's sense of humor. "Ah, they're the cream of the crop."

Bill beamed with pride as he put an arm around Gus—who didn't seem to mind Bill touching him in the least. "We are."

Bane glanced over Bill's head at Weston. "Been a long time, brother."

"It has," said Weston, remaining in place. He wasn't much of a hugger. Bane wasn't, either.

Bill looked between the men. "You're brothers?"

"Served together," said Weston, knowing Bill would understand, as he'd served too.

Bill nodded. "Most of the guys I served with are dead now. They were part of the government's testing too."

Bane cast Weston a questioning look. Weston tapped into a mental path shared by those like him. *LSD testing, back in Vietnam. This here is the famous Wild Bill.*

Bane glanced back at Bill. *The mechanical elephant rider?*

One and the same. DARPA had tried to

place mechanical elephants in the jungles of Vietnam in hopes it would help the fight. It didn't. They were a hot mess. And Bill had been brave enough to scale up one and ride it like a bucking bronco. When Casey had told him the story, Weston had found it amusing and he could totally picture the crazy little guy doing it. He could bet Bill gave the government a run for their money. Part of Weston felt bad for Bill and Gus. After all, they too were victims of the government.

What about the other one? Bane moved his attention to Gus. *He okay?*

I can hear you both, said Gus on their same mental pathway, and from the look on Bane's face, surprising the shit out of him.

Bane's lips drew into a thin line. *Interesting.*

"You have a place set up for us?" asked Weston, no longer bothering with the mental pathway.

Bane nodded. "We should get a move-on. Shit has been heating up around here lately."

"I heard about the attack at the docks. Ever figure out what caused all the carnage?" Weston was uneasy about being in the area at all. He had a long-standing history of losing control. He didn't need anyone else giving his shifter side any more ideas.

"No. From my understanding, the I-Ops and PSI don't know, either," replied Bane. It didn't surprise Weston that Bane knew what was going on at each branch, despite being thought dead for the longest time by both. Weston knew better. He'd known Bane was alive the entire time. They'd escaped together. "Though word in the paranormal underground is it's one of us."

"An Outcast?" questioned Weston. It made sense. Most of the Outcasts were either created by scientists using straight animal DNA, or such huge quantities of existing supernatural DNA, that it had all gotten away from them in the end, making monsters instead of heroes.

"You hear anything on your end?"

asked Bane.

Weston shook his head. "Just that whatever has been going on is bad. And that it left one of the I-Ops yanking his mate out of here and making her close her business."

Bane paused as they headed in the direction of a large SUV. Bill and Gus stayed close. That was good. Weston didn't want to tell Casey he lost them. Bane cleared his throat. "That wouldn't have happened to have been a brothel for the supernatural, would it?"

"I think so. Why?"

"It was a happening place," said Bane, looking far off in thought for a minute. "A good place to go to get your needs met by women you knew you wouldn't accidentally kill during sex."

Weston's throat tightened as he thought about Bane's past. The man had lost control during sex, and the woman he'd been with had paid the price. It hadn't been his fault. The damn scientists had forced the sex act to occur, wanting to study the effects of a mating. They had wanted to see what one of their prized were-gorillas would do and how difficult it might be to create one naturally through birth. They had no clue that they'd just sent a human woman to her death or that what they'd done would forever scar their creation—Bane.

Bane hated what they'd made him. Hated that he'd come out the other side a were-gorilla. A lot of the men in their group were more than your garden-variety shifter. The scientists back then had been going through a strange phase of wanting to try out new possible shifter types. Some Outcasts were able to shift into birds, marine life, polar bears, and alligators— hell, just about anything one could think of. And all of them were screwed up because of it.

Damn scientists.

Bane straightened his shoulders. "The place just reopened around a week ago. Word on the street is it's under new ownership. Still caters to supernaturals."

"You going to try it out?" Weston wondered where Bane was going with this.

His friend shrugged. "Maybe. It's getting close to that time for me."

Weston knew what time that was. He was teetering on the edge of it himself. If he didn't shift and have sex soon, didn't matter the order, it would get ugly and fast. Bane had even less control. Weston motioned to Bill and Gus for them to get into the SUV. They did.

He then turned his attention to Bane. "Listen, Gus, the weird one who can talk on our mental path, says I need to be here. That my mate is in danger."

Bane's eyes widened. "You didn't mention that in your call."

With good reason. Weston wasn't about to sound the alarms when he wasn't sure he even had anything to actually sound them over. It was big enough that he'd called in a favor from Bane, pulling Bane out of hiding. "Because I don't have a mate."

Bane tipped his head. "I'm not

following."

"Gus seems to think I do and that she's in danger. Casey believes him," said Weston, setting down a bag.

"Do you?"

He shrugged. "I don't know. Maybe."

"But?" Bane lifted the bag. "What are you leaving out?"

"My head is a mess."

Bane stiffened. "The dreams back?"

"Dreams never left," answered Weston honestly.

"I'm sorry, brother. I am."

Weston shrugged. "It is what it is. I can't do anything to change it. Though lately my signals are getting crossed or something. I'm not getting clear pictures or feelings. My dreams are pretty much a hot mess."

"They hinting at a mate?" asked Bane, hope in his dark gaze.

Weston sighed. "I don't know. Maybe. I haven't shifted in forever and a fucking day and I need to get laid." Weston cracked his knuckles. "Bad."

"Let's get these two to the safe house and we can swing by the club," said Bane, loading the bag into the back of the SUV. "The new owners are supernatural and so are the workers—that's all I know so far. We'll get our rocks off and then be able to focus on this mate thing."

"And if the nut job is right?" asked Weston, his gut tight. "How do I explain to my mate when I meet her that I didn't come right away to help her because I was too busy making a paid bootie call?"

Bane exhaled slowly and then cast him a hard look. "You can't explain jack crap to her if you meet her, lose control and rip her head off because you denied your beast side and the alpha side of you too long. Hard to state your case to a dead person."

"Fair point." Weston exhaled, understanding Bane's words were correct. In his current state of mind, Weston wouldn't be any good to anyone. Dealing with Bill and Gus had left him even more on edge. He was hanging by a thread. He wouldn't be worth a damn right now. Not until he shifted and did something about putting too long between sexual releases. Unfortunately, he'd waited too long that jerking off just wouldn't be enough now. He made a mental note to buy more girlie mags to prevent the same thing from happening in the future. "Better to beg forgiveness?"

"Than ask permission," finished Bane, shutting the back of the SUV. Bane stood there a moment and then surprised Weston by grabbing him and giving him a manly hug.

Weston returned it and Bane released him.

"Enough, or people will think we're a couple or something," said Bane with a shaky laugh. Both men were fighting their emotions. They'd been through a lot together.

"You're not my type," said Weston with a cock-sure smile. "I like blondes."

Bill leaned his head out of the backseat window. "Are you two coming or are you gonna make out? We want ice cream. Ooh, and peanut butter and jelly sandwiches. Stat."

Weston had to temper his breathing for fear he really would kill the little guy. "It takes all of me not to rip his head off."

Bane laughed again. "Nah. He's not that bad."

"The Bane I remember would have already killed him," said Weston.

Bane shrugged. "Spent some time with monks. Did wonders for my self-restraint. Also, I get really bad heartburn off guys full of drugs, and that little man smells like a walking weed plant."

Chapter Three

Paisley Addiks did her best to fade away into the shadows of the smoky sex club. This wasn't her first time visiting the establishment. She'd been something of a regular there up until a few weeks ago. Everything had changed since then. Gone was the safe feeling that had once blanketed the place. Now a sinister note hung in the air, as if warning the occupants that anything could and probably would happen.

No matter how ominous the atmosphere was, Paisley didn't have a choice. She had to be there. She needed to refuel herself with the sexual energy that radiated from every corner of the place and she needed a lead on her missing friend.

She'd been trying for weeks to gain entrance to the club. Once she'd been able to walk in with ease, but that was another thing that had changed recently. From what she'd been able to gather so far, one hell of a fight had broken out at the club and then the previous owner left town. Not long after, the employees all left as well, leaving the club boarded over. But that hadn't lasted long. Someone new was running the show now and they were as bad as bad came.

People on the street had warned Paisley to stay away. To just forget about her missing friend and find other ways to sate the hunger she seemed to always carry. She knew she should heed the warnings, but she had to know what happened to her friend. She just couldn't walk away from the area without finding out the truth.

She didn't want to be noticed by the smarmy men frequenting the establishment. Or the women who seemed too happy to be surrounded by them. There were a few men there who were servicing women. Not as many men as women, though. The men employed there wore the smallest of covers for their man bits, while showing off the rest of their bodies in all their naked glory—backside included.

Instead of turning her on, as she suspected was their purpose, she just sort of turned her nose up at them. They weren't her type, whatever her type was.

"Get through tonight and then you can figure out a new game plan," she said softly to herself, continuing in the direction of one of the hallways. She just needed to recharge her batteries, so to speak. To soak in the essence of sex that filled the place. She wasn't entirely sure what she was, only that she was more than human, and that more than human side of herself left her craving sexual energy, but so far, never craving the act itself. Maybe she was broken. She wasn't sure. She didn't care.

The club had always worked to satisfy her cravings, until very recently. Now she never seemed full. The place was a high end, underground sex club. There was no better way to describe it. To the outside world, it was simply a private club that catered to the elite. No one questioned what went on behind closed doors. Paisley did. Her friend had gone missing while working there and Paisley intended to find out where Galiena, or Gale as she was known around the clubs, was. Where everyone was and who the hell these new people all were, because they certainly weren't the people who ran and operated the club.

Paisley understood the draw of the brothel. Understood the lure of why Gale would want and ultimately need to be there. Gale also needed sexual energy to survive. Though Gale's needs ran deeper than Paisley's. Gale needed actual sex to keep going. Simple sexual energy wouldn't do for her. It wasn't enough. She needed to complete the act. The club had given Gale what she needed—a safe place to feed, to recharge and get her needs met. Or, at least the club used to offer that. Foolishly, Paisley had believed that when Gale found others like herself, others who needed sex to survive, and who weren't what anyone would label straight humans, that Gale would be safe.

Not true.

Not true at all.

Gale was special. So was Paisley. Unique, as Gale had always put it. They'd figured out as much when they were in their late teens, not that they were exactly far from the age now. Paisley felt worldly. As if she'd seen and done more than most girls in their early twenties. And she had. Then again, she wasn't anything like most girls.

At least Gale had made her feel less alone. Like less of a freak. But now Gale was gone. So was everyone else that

Paisley had met through her friend. There was no sign of the redheaded woman who owned the place—Jinx. Though, word on the street was that Jinx cleared out of town and had moved her people with her. But not Gale. Paisley would have known if Gale went too. Gale would have told her. They were that close.

Jinx had always been kind to Paisley, even offering her a job at the club. One that wouldn't mean she had to service anyone sexually, but that would let her serve drinks, letting her be around the sexual energy, soaking it in. Paisley hadn't been able to bring herself to do it. Doing so was like admitting defeat—not that sneaking around in brothels was any better. All she wanted to be was normal. She wanted a normal life, a normal job, and to stop having the urges. Instead, she'd let Gale sneak her in through one of the hidden entrances and she'd simply hang around in the hallways, gathering what was needed to make her feel rejuvenated again. Not an ounce more.

And she never had to touch anyone.

But lately the hunger wasn't sated like it used to be. Simply being near all the sex in the club wasn't doing it for her anymore and she had no one to talk to about it. There wasn't a support group for sex-addicted supernaturals. At least, none that she was aware of. Though, there were a lot of things out there that weren't human and they probably did have get-togethers.

She wasn't sure she wanted to take part in them.

"How much for you?" a short, thin man asked, his eyes beady and his lips too narrow. He put a hand up on the wall near her, blocking her path. "What are you supposed to be? The girl next door? Bet that sells well."

Paisley pressed an artificial grin to her face, trying to look somewhat pleasant. The idea of the man touching her made her skin crawl. When Jinx had been running the place, men like this one wouldn't have been allowed in. They hadn't catered to scumbags, and this guy seemed like one. "I'm taken. See the front desk for who might be available."

He pulled a toothpick from his pocket and tossed it between his lips. "Damn shame. I haven't banged a succubus in a while. You lot always give it good."

Succubus? Gale had tossed the term about more than once too, hinting that Paisley might be at least part succubus. "What makes you think I'm a succubus?"

He sniffed the air, his beady eyes flickering to gold quickly before a forked tongue appeared out of his mouth. "I smell it."

She didn't scream at the sight of him, which was saying a lot. She'd seen some freaky crap at the club, but he was new. "W-what are you?"

"Snake shifter," he said, touching the front of his pants. "Wanna see?"

She squared her shoulders and looked past him, acting as if she had a client there, waiting. She waved in the other direction. "Coming!"

The man glanced over his shoulder and then back at her. "When you're done, find me."

"Sure," she said, hurrying away from him as fast as she could. She ducked down another hall and exhaled, thankful to be rid of him. A shiver raced down her spine and she had to take a deep, calming breath. She knew better than to show fear in the club. Gale had explained as much to her more than once.

Fear excites a lot of the clients.

Several more people walked past her and paused, looking her over. They continued on, but when two women approached, arm in arm, they paused, coming to a stop before her. The woman on the left had a completely shaved head and a dog collar on. The tag read "bitch." She had on a barely there top made of mesh, showing her nipples and breasts. Her skirt slung low on her hips. Tattoos marked the skin at the point where the skirt started. There were faint bite marks all over the woman's body. Some looked fresh, others looked to be from long ago. None looked as though they'd been pleasant to receive. But Paisley had seen some weird stuff in her time and knew some people got off on pain and biting. Some things required it.

The woman's eyes flashed to black and she smiled, showing fang. Paisley didn't shake or quiver in fear. She'd learned years ago that scary stuff of nightmares was real. In some ways, she was included in the mix. This woman didn't scare her—much.

Vampire, thought Paisley. She'd bumped into a few in her time. Most of the run-ins had been uneventful. Some hadn't. Gale had been with her for all of them. There had been a point in her life when Paisley hadn't known things like vampires existed. Seemed like another life. Now she knew about a lot of things that went bump in the night. Things that would terrify normal people.

Things that sometimes still managed to scare her.

Like the snake-shifter guy.

She shuddered.

Swallowing hard, Paisley did her best to pretend she was supposed to be there in hopes the women would simply lose interest in her and move on. No such luck. The bald woman eyed her, and the woman's friend, who looked fairly normal compared to the other one with the shaved head, grinned. No fangs showed. Of course, that didn't mean the woman wasn't a vampire.

Paisley tried to get an idea of what the other woman was, but she couldn't get a good read. That had always been something Gale was better at. Gale had always seemed the stronger of the two of them in terms of what she brought to the table. And now she was nowhere to be found.

A nagging pit returned deep inside Paisley's stomach as she looked at the women before her. She couldn't help but feel as if they knew something about Gale's disappearance. That they were somehow connected. The one with the shaved head reached out quickly and snatched hold of Paisley's upper arm, squeezing firmly, drawing a gasp as she did.

"What have we here?" she asked, her accent sounding Eastern European.

Her companion laughed. "A little virginal stray puppy."

Paisley stiffened. "I'm not a virgin."

The women laughed.

"Liar," said the vampire. "We can smell innocence on you and something else?"

Her friend leaned in, blatantly sniffing her. "What is that?"

"Succubus?" asked the vampire, seeming surprised. "How does a succubus stay a virgin?"

Paisley tried to pry her arm free to no avail. "I need to go."

"Why are you here?" asked the other. "You aren't one of those leftovers, are you? From the other owner."

"What do you know of Jinx?" asked Paisley, drawing suspicious looks from both women.

"The better question is, what do you?" asked the vampire, sneering, tightening her hold on Paisley. "We'll take you before the boss and you can answer his questions. I'm sure he has a ton for you. And he likes virgins. Though you won't be one for long once you meet him."

"Let go of me," said Paisley, only managing to get her arm squeezed harder. "I'll go. I shouldn't have come here. I just needed...."

"Needed what?" asked the vampire as she pushed in closer, her face close to Paisley's. "Tell me or you'll tell the boss."

"I'll go."

"Oh, you'll stay now," said the vampire with a laugh. She hissed and then made a move to bite Paisley, but stopped just shy of doing so, laughing harder as Paisley tensed. Tears wanted to fall, but she held tight, refusing to let the woman wearing a tag that summed her up see her cry. They pushed on Paisley, forcing her to back up more and more, and before she realized it, they had backed her into a room. One of the rooms reserved for servicing clients.

They laughed as they slammed the door shut, locking her in. Paisley hit the door, pounding on it, but they didn't open it. Their laughter was loud enough to hear through the closed door.

"Don't worry, sweetheart," one shouted. "The boss will be in soon enough to keep you company."

Chapter Four

"This is a bad idea." Weston and Bane stood outside the sex club. Leaving Gus and Bill alone at a safe house wasn't sitting well with him. They'd taken an unnatural interest in the pool at the safe house. "What if we go back and they've drowned?"

Bane cast him a sideways glance. "Then you have two less things to worry about the rest of this trip."

He rolled his eyes, finding no humor in the idea Bill and Gus would drown. "You know what I mean."

"They're grown men," reminded Bane,

but Weston wasn't so sure of that. The two seemed like man-children to him. He'd even called Casey to ask his opinion and the guy had thought they'd be fine on their own so long as no one left them access to keys or a car. Weston wasn't so sure.

"Um, you met them. Anything about them say they were grown yet?" asked Weston, still concerned. "We should call and check in. I left a burner cell with them."

"For a guy who threatens to eat them non-stop, you're very protective," said Bane, giving him a knowing look as if he suspected all along that Weston had a soft spot for the two stooges. "They'll be fine. They've got ice cream, peanut butter and jelly sandwiches, and some DVDs I stocked in the place. They're all good. And I even told them to wait thirty minutes after eating before they swim."

"Oh good, I should have remembered that." Weston wasn't used to palling around with humans anymore. It had been a long time since he'd been what one would term human, and he made a point after his change to cut ties with most. He'd been on his own before he'd joined the service, his mother passing when he was just a boy and his father totally unknown. He didn't have family beyond that, and if he did, he didn't know them. Somewhere in his family tree there were supernaturals, but he'd more than likely never know how or where. He accepted that. Didn't like it much, but it was what it was.

Bane snorted and put his hand on Weston's shoulder, giving it a squeeze. "I was kidding. Relax. They're adults. They're fine. Now, let's handle your issue and mine."

"You too?" he asked, wishing he had the same level of control over himself that Bane seemed to. "I may need to visit those monk friends of yours."

"You wouldn't last five minutes," said Bane, grinning as he rapped on the door to the club. "Some of those monks could kick my ass."

Weston snorted and then tipped his head. "Seriously?"

"Yeah, they were mostly shifters."

"That explains a lot."

A big guy who was probably supposed to look intimidating and be the muscle opened the door. The man made a half-hearted attempt to appear tough and then seemed to think better of it. Smart guy.

"Enter," the man said, sounding as if he was forcing his voice to be deeper than it was, and stepping aside to let them pass.

Amateur.

Weston was first in. He sniffed the air, sensing something was off, but he couldn't put his finger on what. With as long as he'd been around, he'd spent a fair amount of time seeking out brothels that catered to the supernatural. It was sort of required when you didn't have a mate and weren't a guy a human girl could really handle. As was the case with Weston. He could go a couple of months between sexual releases now and he was thankful, because he tended to be a little bit too much for even supernatural, paid professionals. He did his best to calm his alpha side. It rarely worked.

Bane cast him a sideways glance. Did he sense something was off at the brothel too?

If so, he said nothing as two scantily clad women approached them, each holding a tray of drinks. The women were sexy, just like all the women were who were employed in places like this. Normally, Weston would have either snagged one of the welcome girls to fuck or placed his order then and there. He did neither. He simply watched them as they came to a stop. The blonde smiled up at Weston, pushing her chest out as she did. "Drink for the shifter?"

She was probably a magik of some sort. They were decent at guessing what supernaturals were if they were trained well enough to spot them. One of the drinks was smoking and Weston had to wonder if that was healthy for anyone—

immortal or not. Another looked to be a Bloody Mary, complete with actual blood from the smell of it. More than likely on hand for vampires or other supernaturals who preferred human blood in place of tomato juice. He wasn't one of them.

He also wasn't one for frills when it came to what he drank. He liked it simple —straight liquor and beer. He reached for the beer and noticed Bane wasn't biting on a drink even with how insistent the redhead near him was.

Bane held up a hand signaling he wasn't interested in having a drink. "No. Thank you, though."

The woman pouted her lips and swayed her hips back and forth slightly, as if to entice Bane. "Then tell me what you do want."

Bane thumbed to Weston. "My friend requires company of the female persuasion. For now, I'll just watch."

She shook her head, looking Bane over slowly. "Shame, but if being a voyeur is your thing, we cater to that too. Are you sure you don't want a little something more? I'd be happy to give it to you."

"No. I'm good. Thank you for the offer."

Weston stared at his friend and then linked on their mental path. *I thought you needed to handle the urges?*

I do, but first I want to look around. Do you sense it?

Sense what? asked Weston, already knowing what Bane would say. Clearly, he sensed something was off too.

Shit.

Weston was hoping to just have a quick fuck and be on with his night and get going with the search for the mysterious berries-and-cream girl. Of course the night would come with strings attached. Why wouldn't it?

The blonde gave a sultry smile as she reached out and touched the beer he was holding. "Tell me what type of woman you want and what kind of experience you're looking for. We have it all. And I mean all of it. We are here to assure your fantasies are met."

Weston handed her the beer and then stopped in mid-movement as the smell of fresh berries and cream smacked him right in the face. He froze. It was her. She was here. He was sure of it. That or he was dreaming while being fully awake.

Anything was possible anymore.

The smell roused the bear in him, making sure the man paid attention.

Of course you perk up when berries come into play, assface, he thought, more to his inner beast than himself.

His cock hardened at a shocking rate. He sniffed the air without bothering to try to make the action look like one a human would do. There was no point in subterfuge. He was surrounded by those who understood what he was. By those who made their living catering to his alpha needs.

Bane nudged him. "Weston?"

"Do you smell that?" he asked, his pulse speeding and his breathing moving to match it. Who was the owner of the smell? Was she really here or was he just imagining it? Had his mind finally snapped? Would he be left like Gus, who had similar gifts to him but was so very obviously broken?

"Smell what?" asked Bane, stepping closer.

"Berries and cream," replied Weston, on automatic pilot as he turned in a circle, looking around, trying to figure out if it was real or in his head.

"I don't smell anything but sex. The place is rich with it," said Bane. "You okay?"

He waved a hand at his friend in a dismissive manner. He couldn't worry about Bane now. Not when he was so close to the woman who had been haunting his dreams. He had to find her. He had to see her. Had to put a face to the smell. Mostly, he had to see if she was real or if he'd finally cracked.

He made a move to enter the club more, but the blonde blocked his path. He didn't want a drink or to make a selection. He wanted the owner of the smell. He could have moved the blonde with ease, but he didn't touch a woman that way, not unless she was wielding a weapon or shifting to try to kill him. That had happened a number of times in his long life. Bad guys weren't reserved to just men. They came in the form of women too. A lesson he'd learned the hard way and he had the scars to prove it.

"Who is that?" he asked, sniffing the air more, the smell of berries and cream mixing with something else. Was it fear?

The need to find the owner of the scent and protect her was nearly all consuming. And he knew without a shadow of a doubt the scent belonged to a female. Not just any woman, either. The one he was supposed to find. The woman he'd dreamed of. He'd stake his life on it.

The blonde pressed closer to him, the tray of drinks beginning to wobble. There was concern in her eyes. "Now, now, what do you smell?"

"Perfection," he said, unsure why the word popped out. "I want her. I want the one I smell. I'll triple whatever you ask for her. I want her now."

"Weston, brother," said Bane, concern in his voice. "You all right?"

He stared around the dimly lit club, his gaze searching each of the groupings of people. Some were petting one another and another group was engaged in oral sex out in the open. In the back of Weston's mind, he thought about the clubs he'd been to in the past that were run on the level. Very few of those permitted such acts to be done in the open area. But he didn't care. All he wanted right now was for the woman who smelled like berries and cream to show herself.

He moved past the woman at the door, despite her protests. Weston walked closer to the groups of people. If anyone was touching the woman he was smelling, he'd rip their fucking heads off. She was his.

Mine?

He paused, realizing he was sweating. Someone was touching him, but why? He looked at his forearm and found Bane's hand there, grabbing him. Bane locked gazes with him.

"Weston, we should go, something isn't right with you," he said in a voice that sounded as if he was working hard at keeping calm.

Shaking his head, Weston stood his ground. He'd fight Bane to stay if it came down to it. It would be a hell of a match-up, but he didn't care. He wasn't leaving. Not without the woman. "No."

Bane's brows met, but he said nothing more as he released Weston's arm. He stepped back. "Do what you must. I've got your back."

That was all Weston needed to hear. He pushed into the club deeper. Vaguely, he heard a bit of a commotion behind him, but he didn't turn to see what it was. He kept going into the club more, drawn to the hallway on the far side of the room. The moment he stepped into it, he froze. There was a woman with a shaved head there smelling of vampire, and another woman with her, smelling of the same. It was faint but there. Maybe newly turned. His hard-on began to die as if someone had thrown cold water on him.

Had he been attracted to hardcore vamps?

He was about to turn to walk away when the smell of berries and cream hit him again, nearly knocking him back. Growling, he rushed forward and the vampires turned, their eyes wide. "Where is she?"

"Who?" they asked in unison, attempting to sport innocent looks and failing miserably.

Sniffing the air, he felt his beast begin to win and knew without needing a mirror that his eyes had shifted colors to a deep dark brown, bordering on black. His nostrils flared as the burning need to find and lay claim to the owner of the scent continued to assault him without mercy. He shook, his claws itching to emerge from his fingertips. He would tear the vampires limb from limb if they didn't give him who he wanted.

The shaved-head one smirked and then licked her lips. The vampires shared a glance and smiled wide as if they were up to no good. "Alpha male shifter, hmm?"

"Yes," he managed, but only barely. Fur appeared on his forearms and his clothing felt tight. Too tight.

"Weston," said Bane. "Control it, man, or you will lose it in here."

The vampire with the shaved head continued to smile as she crooked her finger, drawing him closer. "We have the perfect special going on right now. The virgin prize package. I bet that is what you want, you big, strong, alpha male."

He paid her little mind, his head full of the scent of the object of his obsession. "Where is she?"

She tapped the door near them both. "Right through here, but be warned, she'll play the part perfectly. Be sure you play yours. Take her hard, rough and dirty."

Bane grabbed him roughly. "This is unwise."

He shook free of his friend and glared at him.

Bane sighed. "Don't make me knock you out and drag you out of a whorehouse."

"I'm good," said Weston through teeth that were bordering on shifting form.

Bane lifted a dark brow. "Really?"

The vampires converged on Bane, petting him and smiling, pulling him from Weston and the doorway. The one with the shaved head motioned to Weston. "Go. Enjoy."

He opened the door, unable to wait any longer. Once inside the dimly lit room he was hit full-on with the smell he desired. He staggered and had to regain his footing, his breathing harsh, his mind racing. He looked over near the bed and found a young woman there, her dark eyes wide with fear as she pressed her back to the wall, looking as though she hoped she could blend in with the wallpaper. She was small in stature, maybe five-five at most, which was tiny in comparison to himself.

Really fucking tiny.

Her large brown eyes were wide with fear and set in a perfect heart-shaped face. Full lips pulled into a gasp and she touched the back of her hand to her mouth. She wasn't dressed like the rest of the women in the club—in barely anything. This woman wore a small white t-shirt that pulled against her ample breasts before accenting her waist. The old jean skirt she had on was frayed at the bottom as if made from an actual pair of jeans. Weston couldn't remember a time in his life when he'd found such a simple choice of attire so damn hot. Long waves of curly brown hair fell over the woman's shoulders, nearly touching her waist. He could hear his heart hammering as he stared at her, his bear riding his thoughts and actions, making hit hard for him to concentrate.

He knew this woman. How did he know her?

The beast continued to push at him, demanding he give in to his baser needs.

Demanding he take the prize before him, to hell with finding his mate on this night. All he could think about was the woman with him now.

Chapter Five

Paisley couldn't take her eyes off the man who had entered the room. He was huge. Well over six and half feet. There didn't look to be any part of him that wasn't solid muscle. The two wenches who had tossed her into the room hadn't mentioned the boss coming would be hot. Maybe the hottest guy she'd ever laid eyes on. He leaked power and authority all over the room. She should have been terrified of him. Of what he was about to do to her, but she wasn't.

Whatever she carried in her, whatever had been forcing her to fill up on sexual energy but never permitted her to take it any further, seemed to click into high gear —making her crave the man before her as much as she did.

Maybe more.

With a gasp she moved away from the safety of the wall and the other corner of the room, wanting closer to the man. There was something feral about him. Like he wanted to ravish her and pound into her until she lost consciousness. The idea sounded just fine by her.

Wait—what was she thinking? *Run. Get away. Shout.*

Her body did none of the above. She found herself licking her lips, her gaze raking over him slowly. "H-How big are you?"

He cocked his head to one side, his nearly black gaze snapping to her face. "Bigger than you can probably handle."

"We'll see," she returned, shocking herself even more. What was wrong with her? Why did she suddenly sound like Gale whenever Gale was servicing men?

Every warning her friend had ever given her crashed into her at once.

Be careful if you feel like you can't stop. You could kill someone. Make sure the man can handle it. Make sure he can handle what you are.

As she looked over the man in the room —the boss—she knew without a shadow of a doubt he could handle her. He could more than handle her. Paisley stepped out into the room further, lifting her head, her chin tipped upwards as false confidence seemed to emanate from her. "Are we doing this?"

The man touched the front of his jeans, his long, hard erection outlined there for her to see. "Oh, we're most certainly doing this."

She had to hide her smile. She wasn't the type who just threw herself at a man. Why in the world was she doing it now? Why with this one? He was a jerk who was the boss of that bitch vampire and her friend. More than that, he probably had s o m e t h i n g   t o   d o   w i t h   G a l e ' s

Mandy M. Roth

disappearance. Her rational mind screamed at her to leap on this man, claw his eyes out and demand answers. That wasn't what happened at all. Her mind seemed to have a thought process all its own. One she found herself more and more willing to go along with as the man yanked his t-shirt over his head and cast it aside.

He stood there, watching her from unnaturally dark eyes, his upper body bare. Every rippling muscle there for her to see, taunting her as if saying "come touch me, come feel how hard I am." Her mouth watered as she covered the distance between them, each step she took confirming what was going to happen. She was going to have sex with him, and odds were she was going to love every second of it.

Simply being in the room with him was a rush of sexual energy unlike any she'd ever experienced before. It made her feel alive, refreshed, and it left her craving more. It would be easy to become addicted to him, to what he seemed to radiate—pure masculinity and raw need.

His wavy, dark brown hair hung just past his shoulders, adding to his sex appeal. A decent dusting of facial hair covered his strong jawline and she found herself reaching up, wanting to make contact with his face.

He bent his head, his breathing rapid. It was then she noticed his hands were out to his sides as if he was fighting the need to make contact with her. Fighting the same pull she felt to him.

"Can I touch you?" she asked, feeling more like her old self and less like a wanton, sex-crazed junkie.

"Hell yeah," he said, sounding labored. "Touch me all over, baby."

"Paisley," she told him, blurting out her name without thinking anything of it. Deep down she knew she should ask about her friend. Find out what this man might know, but that wasn't what came out of her mouth. "Or my name could be whatever you want it to be."

His lips quirked, and darn it if he didn't get even sexier. "Your name is Paisley?"

She nodded.

"Real name or club name?" he asked, easing closer to her, taking her hand in his and bringing it to his cheek. He then traced her hand down his neck to his upper chest. His skin was blazing hot to the touch. As she soaked in the sight of him there, his darkened eyes, his rapid breathing, his hot skin, she bit her lower lip.

"Shifter?" she asked, unsure what made her lean the way of guessing shifter rather than another type of supernatural.

He nodded. "Bear."

"You're a bear-shifter?" she asked, surprised. She'd never met or even heard of one of them.

"Answer my question first, baby," he said, trailing her hand lower on his torso. "Is that your real name?"

"It is," she said, gasping as her fingers skimmed over the start of a line of hair that ran from his bellybutton down into the top of his jeans. "Now answer mine."

"Yes. I'm a bear-shifter. Is that going to be an issue?" he asked, his hands making their way to her hair. He lifted it and brought long strands of it to his face, inhaling deeply. His eyes rolled slightly and he snarled lightly. "Berries and cream."

"What?" she asked, focused more on his abs than his words. His torso had scars on it. They were faint but there all the same. Several tattoos covered parts of him, only adding to his hot factor. She grinned as she noticed one of the tattoos was a tribal bear. She wanted to lean forward and lick him. When she thought harder about where she was and who she was with, she did just that. She licked a line near one of his longer scars.

The man sucked in a big breath and then surprised her by lifting her off her feet, making her yelp. They were suddenly eye-to-eye. His full lips were so close that Paisley did what any self-respecting girl who required sexual energy would do in the situation.

She kissed him.

His mouth opened and before she knew it, he was in control of the kiss. His tongue darted into her mouth and she moaned, hers greeting his. Fire erupted deep within her and she thought she might burn alive if he didn't hurry up and get things moving faster and soon.

She ran her hands over his shoulders, their kiss growing faster and more heated. She bit at his lower lip as her legs wrapped around his waist, their bodies pressed tightly together. He smelled like a man should. Like the wild—the forest, the earth, the air.

Everything about him excited her, demanding she draw all she could from him. He appeared willing to give in to her needs. Very willing.

Paisley stopped caressing him long enough to pull her shirt over her head. Her hair got tangled up in it for a moment, but she managed to free herself, her bra-covered breasts rubbing in the man's face as she did. Her nipples hardened and he growled, catching one in his mouth and biting lightly through the lace, turning her on more.

She feared for a split second that she might actually go up in flames if he kept going, kept turning her on more and more. She caught the sides of his face. "Have a name or do I call you boss?"

He waggled his brows. "Boss works."

Something loud hit the door and Paisley jerked in the man's arms, grabbing hold of him, deep down knowing he represented safety, despite being the leader of the mean girls. He moved his hands around her, holding her up by her backside.

"What was that?" she asked, her gaze going toward the door.

He toyed with her nipple through her bra once more. "I don't fucking care if the world is ending. I just want this. You. Here and now."

Her attention returned to him and she met his gaze, her chest tightening, her body aching for more of him. The need reflected in his gaze moved her. She unfastened her bra in front, allowing her breasts to be free, there for the taking. And did he ever take. He used one hand to hold her up and the other to cup a breast as he kissed it, sucking on her nipple. Each swipe of his mouth left her pussy contracting as if it knew what was coming next. She wasn't even sure what was going to happen next, but her body was.

She closed her eyes a second, enjoying the rush of sexual energy moving through her. She'd never felt so alive. So free. So wild. She loved every moment of it.

He walked her in the direction of the wall and then pressed her against it, using his body to pin hers in place. He reached down and edged her skirt up more, his fingers skimming over her panties. She tensed as he eased the material aside, his finger finding its way to her slit.

He kissed her mouth as he touched her wet, hot entrance. She tried to move her hips more, to force herself onto his finger but he was too powerful and had full control over their movements. He froze, his tongue wrapped around hers.

He stopped the kiss but kept his face where it was, his finger at her entrance, his body pressed against hers. "You're a virgin?"

"Yes," she said, trying again to wiggle onto his finger with no luck.

"A real virgin?" he asked, his voice raising somewhat.

She paused. "What other kind is there?"

He remained in place. "Shit. I thought when they said you were the virgin prize package they just meant you were some girl pretending to be one and playing the part. Pretending to be one and actually being one are two different things."

She pushed at his chest, wanting more than he was giving. "Boss guy, fuck me. Now."

His entire body tensed and then he took his finger from her entrance, leaving her in a state of wanting. "Not like this."

"Oh, this is perfect. Do it!" she demanded, tugging on him this time. He was a lot like trying to move semi-truck using nothing but a pinkie finger. It wasn't happening.

"Paisley, I want to. Trust me, I do, but I have to live with myself come morning," he said, drawing his face back from her slightly. It was then she noticed his eyes were no longer dark. They were a royal blue that seemed to suit him even better.

She tipped her head, her fingers going to just under his eye. "Your eyes are blue now."

He nodded and then his gaze narrowed. He lifted a lock of her hair and smelled it again. Before she knew it, he had her set gently on her feet and was turning her away from him. She'd seen enough people having sex in the club to know all the positions. If he wanted it this way, fine. Just so long as he finished what he started. When he did nothing more, she looked over her shoulder at him.

"Boss?" she questioned, noticing then

his eyes were wide and a sheen of sweat was now covering his brow.

"Oh shit," he said softly.

"What is it?"

"The scent, the hair, the profile from behind," he said, his voice steady even as additional sweat beaded on him, this time his chest. "It's you."

"What?" she asked, no longer following. "Boss, you're not making a lot of sense."

He ran a hand over his face. "I ran to a whorehouse in hopes of heading off my behavior before I met my mate, and instead I walk right into her and nearly lose control anyway."

"Okay, you've totally lost me now." She turned to face him.

He paused and then his expression narrowed more. "Wait a minute. Why the hell are you here in a whorehouse?"

She stiffened, disliking what he was implying. It wasn't as if he was above reproach in the situation. His halo wasn't sparkly or shiny by any stretch of the imagination. "You're here, why can't I be here?"

"Were you just waiting here in this den of debauchery for any old guy to show up and punch your V-card?" he demanded, moving toward her, his chest heaving.

"Den of debauchery? Are you for real?" She took a step back and put up her hands. "My V-card? Boss guy, are you on drugs?"

He waved a hand in the air for a moment looking as though he were swatting flies. "Virgin dance card. It's what the kids today are calling it."

She couldn't stop the laugh that bubbled free from her. She covered her mouth and kept laughing. "Virgin dance card? Seriously? I think you were misinformed."

"This is funny?" He crossed his arms over his massive chest. "Explain why you are here."

Huffing, she put her hands on her hips. "You run the place. Explain that."

"I what?" he asked, appearing confused. "I don't run the place."

"They said the boss was coming in and he'd take my virginity," she said, referring to the vampire bitch and her friend. "I thought you'd be a hideous beast of a man. Now I realize you're just a jerk."

He blinked, a show of surprise on his face. "Oh, I'm a beast all right, baby. I'll show you just how much of one I can be later. Now, get your stuff together. We're leaving."

She held firm. "I'm not going anywhere with you, Boss."

He leveled his gaze on her and she had a feeling he'd just toss her over his shoulder if need be. It wouldn't be hard for him. He was huge and powerful. "You most certainly are and the name is Weston, baby. Learn it, because you're stuck with it and me."

She kept her hands on her hips, trying to appear as if she had a chance of winning in the stubborn-streak area. She wasn't so sure she did. He seemed to be a world class champ in the field. "I'm not stuck with anyone or anything. I'm going home. Move."

He caught her around the waist and yanked her to him, making her body heat more. She was torn between slapping him and kissing him.

"You're not setting foot in that club without me," he said, his warm breath skating over her cheek. "No man is to even look at you, let alone touch you. I don't know what the hell you're doing working in a place like this, but it ends this instant. You're coming home with me. Where you belong."

"Excuse you, Boss, erm, Weston," she said, liking the feel of being held by him, but disliking his blanket proclamation. She wasn't one to be owned. No. She'd been on her own for far too long to let some testosterone-driven jackass start calling the shots all of the sudden. "I don't know you. You don't own me. You're not my boss."

He snorted. "Sweetheart, I'm a hell of a lot more than your boss. I'm your mate."

Mate?

Gale and her friends had talked about mates before. They were supernaturals destined for one another. They said the bond between them was instantaneous, as was the attraction. And they joked about how feral and overprotective the males were of their mates. How they bordered on pigheaded jerks and that nature left them acting that way. Something about the inborn need to see to it their mate was protected at all costs, sometimes to the sanity of the mate in question.

This guy had the pigheaded jerk part down pat.

Her mouth opened and then closed again as words failed her. She couldn't be his mate. She didn't even know him. And she hadn't planned to be at the club. She'd just needed to recharge her batteries and couldn't put it off anymore. Then, he'd just wandered into the place and started making out with her. As she thought harder about it, she found her ire rising once more. "Wait a minute, what are you doing in a whorehouse if you're not the owner?"

He stiffened and then released his hold on her, backing up and raising his hands. If his goal was to appear innocent, he failed, miserably. "Now, baby, listen. I told you I'm a bear-shifter, right?"

"You did," she said, eyeing him closely, realizing why he was really there, and it wasn't to save her. He was there for a paid booty call, just like all the other guys who frequented the establishment. "You forgot to mention you were a sleazebag jerk who seeks out sex in clubs and who apparently likes to buy the virgin prize package."

His face reddened. "It's not like that."

"Looks just like that to me, *Boss*." She pointed at him. "And you dared to lecture me."

He kept his hands up. "Baby, listen. Please. I haven't had sex in weeks and I'm overdue, and I was worried if I went searching for you without scratching that itch first, I might hurt you."

She gave him a pointed stare, wondering if he realized how ridiculous his point was. "Does saying it out loud make you realize how stupid it sounds?"

He had the decency to offer a sheepish smile. "Little bit, yeah."

She shook her finger at him in a scolding manner. "Bad bear. Now move. I'm leaving."

He lowered his hands. "Paisley, please. Hear me out."

"Oh, I heard you," she said, shaking her head. "This night keeps getting better and better. Gale is missing. Jinx is gone. Then I need to feed so I show up here hoping to fix that and get tossed and locked in here by some bitch vampire who apparently is going to hand me to her boss. Then my supposed mate shows up in hopes of scratching his itch before he what? Comes to rescue me? Pfft. Right."

"You know Jinx? Asher's mate?" Weston eased closer to her. "Wait, those vampires locked you in here?"

She nodded. "Yes, the vampires locked me in here. And who is Asher?"

His jaw set. "And the vampires told you

they were giving you to their boss?"

"I thought you were him," she said, tugging her skirt down to cover her panties before she tried and failed to fasten her bra. She'd put on enough of a show for Weston. She was done. And she was certainly done with all the nonsense talk of mates. Too many times in her life her hopes had been crushed and she'd learned at an early age that nothing came for free and fairy tales weren't real.

Life was a bitch and she just had to figure out how to best survive it. She didn't need a complication like Weston. Not now. She just needed out of the club and to find Gale. Her friend was missing and she didn't have time for any of this. The more she thought about it all, the more her emotions began to build, threatening to overtake her. She made a move to dart away as the tears threatened to fall.

Weston moved up and touched her hands, stopping her actions. "Paisley, look at me."

She did, even though she didn't want to. The man was a weakness she couldn't afford.

"And you were going to give yourself freely to this boss guy?" he asked, hurt evident in his voice.

She barely knew the man, but even she felt bad for him. She shook her head. "No. I was looking for something to attack him with when you entered. I thought you were him and, I don't know. Something about you made me react differently. I normally only come here to soak up the sexual energy by lingering in the halls. I never participate in the events, obviously. And I never want to. But then you showed up and everything changed. I couldn't think straight. I just wanted you to finish what you'd started." The tears she'd done so well at keeping at bay returned. This time with a vengeance. She broke down and Weston dragged her into his arms.

"Shh, baby, it's okay," he said, holding her close, offering her comfort that she wasn't used to receiving. "No one is going to hurt you now. If the boss guy dares to show his face I'll rip it off and shit down his neck. No one touches my woman. No one. Got it?"

She laughed through her tears and then stilled, thinking about everything he'd said to her. "Wait, you're serious? You think I'm your mate?"

"I know you are," he said matter-of-factly. The resolve he showed moved her, despite how much she wanted to stay hard to it and to him. "I've been dreaming of you for weeks. Then Gus said you were out here and that you needed help and here I am."

"Gus?" she asked, having a hard time following along.

"Long story," he supplied, wiping her cheeks. "Listen, I get you don't know or trust me."

"Oddly enough, I do trust you," she said, shaking her head, shocked at her own behavior. She hadn't survived this long on her own by blindly trusting anyone. "I don't know why."

"Because we're mates," he returned with a wink. He then carefully took each side of her bra and moved them to cover her exposed breasts, fastening them in the center. He didn't try to feel her up or take advantage. Rather, he took care to avoid anything other than being kind and gentle. From the size of him she had to guess that being gentle took a lot of effort on his part.

He bent and grabbed her shirt, appearing stiff in his movements. For some reason, she didn't like seeing him sore or thinking he might be in pain.

"Are you okay?" she asked, touching his back as he was bent.

He groaned, touching the front of his jeans. "Dying a death by way of a massive fucking erection, but I'll be fine. You're what matters here, not me. Let's get you out of here and then we can figure everything out."

"Or," she said, touching his face as he started to stand, her shirt in his hand. She felt bold around him and free. And there was no denying how horny he made her. He called to whatever she carried deep inside her. It wanted free and it wanted him. No use in denying the fact. "We could get the sex part out of the way...."

He closed his eyes. "Paisley, I haven't had sex lately. I'm dangerous to be with. I should be chained for our first encounter. And really, I should do romantic things for you and shit. Whatever it is men do to make women feel special."

She nearly laughed at how out of place he sounded talking about romantic things. "Weston, I understand what you are. I understand what you're telling me, that you're dangerous, but honestly, you seem pretty in control to me right now."

"It's all a show, baby. Trust me, I'm a stone's throw away from fucking you senseless."

She licked her lips, wanting what he was suggesting. "Do it. Fuck me senseless. We have the room and it's made for that type of thing. Let's use it."

Chapter Six

Weston couldn't tear his gaze from Paisley. She was the most beautiful woman he'd ever laid eyes upon. "Baby, I'm a mess of a man. You need to know that upfront. And while that may be true, I'm a big enough man to know how to do right by my woman."

"And you think I'm your woman?" she questioned, her lips in a slight pout. He wanted to kiss them. He resisted in spite of it being one of the hardest things he'd ever done. As much as he wanted to deny who she was to him, he couldn't. He knew in his bones she was his. He didn't need someone else to verify as much. He wasn't as thick-headed as some alpha males, even if others thought he was.

"I know so. I think you do too." He touched the top swell of her left breast, her skin smooth under his fingertips. Didn't she understand what seeing her undone like this was doing to him? Didn't she get how dangerous he could be? "It's why you were willing to give yourself to me when I walked into this room. And before you protest, didn't you just tell me you had no urge to do so before I came along?"

She stilled and then glanced downward, taking a deep breath before meeting his gaze once more, her hand going to his. "I've never wanted anyone to touch me like I want you to touch me. I'll admit that. What does this mean?"

"That your mate is a sleazebag jerk who sought out sex in clubs and who apparently likes to buy the virgin prize packages," he said with a wink.

A smile was his reward, and damn if she didn't look even sexier wearing it. He wanted to touch her lips, run his fingers over them and then sample them once more. "*Boss guy.*"

He grinned. "That's right, baby. Don't forget it."

She took his hand in hers and brought it to her cheek. No additional words were spoken as she planted a tender kiss on each of his knuckles and then took her shirt from his other hand. She eased it over her head and then bent, grabbing his shirt for him. "You should put his on before I lick you again."

"In that case, I'm ripping the damn shirt to bits," he said, drawing her closer to him again. He liked touching her. Liked making contact. He knew deep down that he should hightail it out of the club with her. That something was off there and she wasn't safe, but damn if he didn't dip his head and capture her lips with his own.

He moaned as she opened her mouth to him. It took all he had to drag his mouth from hers, the taste of her still on his lips. He sighed. "We need to go."

"I know," she whispered, remaining near him.

The door to the room burst open and Weston flung himself over Paisley, covering her with his body, protecting her from the shards of wood as they splintered. On high alert, he twisted, coming around fast, his claws emerging, ready to protect what was his.

Paisley.

Her screams echoed around the room as it filled with the motherlode of hybrids. The vampire chicks who had told him about Paisley being in the room were there, grinning from ear to ear. They laughed as several of the large male hybrids moved in on him. Some, like other hybrids Weston had encountered over the last few months, didn't look anything like a human any longer. And all of them smelled rotten, as if they were decaying before his eyes. Whoever or whatever was creating these things hadn't quite gotten the mix right because nothing should smell as they did.

"Tear him to bits, boys," said the shaved head one. "Boss wants the girl. He's got a soft spot for succubus. Try not to mess her up too much. If you do kill her, I'll lie and tell him the shifters did it."

Weston didn't react to her, though he did have to agree with Paisley—the chick was a bitch. He glanced over his shoulder to be sure his woman was covered from the view of prying eyes. She was fully dressed. He eased her back more, keeping her behind him. He didn't want any of these newly formed assholes to take a swing at her.

"Am I late?" Bane appeared in the doorway, looking winded, blood dripping from his mouth. His shirt was missing and his pants were partially undone. Either the fight he'd been in prior to arriving was one hell of a battle or Bane had given in to the temptation of sating his alpha needs. He flashed a wide smile and stared around the room. "Goodie, I didn't miss the party."

"Been up to no good?" asked Weston, noticing his friend's hands were bloody.

"They started it. I was just minding my own business, enjoying a bit of a show and bam, they tried to get in on the action." Bane glanced at Paisley. "And what have you two been up to?"

"Not as much as I'd have liked," said Weston with a snort, his gaze lingering on the enemy. He waited for them to make the first move. For them to show their hand. It didn't take long. A hybrid lunged at Weston and he attacked, going at them with precision and force. These assholes weren't laying a hand on Paisley. Period.

Bane leapt into the room, tackling two of the enemy at one time. He came up off the floor with a head in one hand and an arm of the enemy in the other, a shit-ass-grin on his face.

Weston twisted, slashing a hybrid in half, the blood splatter just missing him fully, hitting the vampires in the face instead. One of them screamed and he shook his head. "Playing with the big boys now, ladies. And really, you're vampires, a little blood and guts should be sexy to you."

The shaved head one glared at him. "Kill him!"

Weston snorted. "Think that is what they're trying to do, precious?"

Bane threw one of the hybrids so hard he went through the wall, cutting a new exit there for them all to take. Weston turned as he heard Paisley gasp. Fear lodged in his throat at what he might find. He was expecting to find her either at the mercy of the bad guys or dead.

He paused mid-swing at another of the men when he watched his mate there, standing on the bed, kicking and landing a good hit on one of the hybrids trying to grab for her. Pride welled in him at the sight of her there, looking like some kind of pint-sized warrior princess.

"Look out!" she shouted, as Weston took a blow to the back of the head and neck, sending him to his knees.

Growling, he pushed up quickly and twisted, dealing with the threat instantly, rendering the hybrid useless. He turned and went at two more, his gaze searching the room for Bane. There was a large pile-up in the corner to the other side of the bed. There had to be at least six hybrids there, piled high on one another.

Weston went at the hybrid near Paisley first, ripping him back and throwing him in the direction of the vampire women. "Catch."

Paisley scrambled off the bed and nearly slipped in a pool of blood and bits on the floor. Weston caught her, dragging her against him, shaking slightly, realizing just how much adrenaline had been running through him and just how worried about her he'd been.

She wasn't shaking in the least, which surprised him. She pushed on his chest. "Your friend needs help."

"Nah, he's fine." Weston said, knowing Bane could take a measly six hybrids. No sooner did the words leave Weston's mouth than Bane came roaring up from the pile, his top half partially shifted into a gorilla, making his mass even more so.

Pulling Paisley against his chest, Weston shielded her from seeing what Bane was about to do—tear the remaining hybrids to bits. And he did. Bane then walked calmly over to the bed, pulled the sheet from it and used it to wipe the excess blood from his face, chest and arms as he returned to human form, seeming as calm as ever.

Guess the monk thing had really worked out for him.

"We should go now," said Bane. "I suspect this was just the tip of it all."

"Agreed," Weston returned, keeping his woman close as he glanced at the vampires, who were scrambling to get out from under the pile of dismembered hybrids. "Tell your boss he isn't laying a finger on her. And make it clear if he comes at me or mine again, I'll come at him. He doesn't want that."

They glared at him as if they wanted to ram hot pokers through his eyes. They probably did. It was a pretty common response to his presence. The one with the shaved head grinned and it was anything but kind. "We know all about you, Outcast. He'll come for you too and the other."

She raked her gaze over Bane.

Bane shrugged. "Ah, he needs to take a number, sweetheart. I've had people coming after me since the day I was born."

She shoved a dead hybrid off her and stood, seemingly unconcerned with facing two shifters on her own. As she glanced upwards, Weston followed her gaze, noticing cameras in the corners of the hallways. They were being watched.

She licked her lips. "The boss and his friends have captured more than one of your kind. In fact, one is so far up a master vampire's ass that he's nothing more than a puppet."

Weston wanted to go at the woman, to rip her head off and show whoever was watching that he wasn't playing around. His gut told him not to. That she was stalling, probably for more backup. Backup he wasn't sure he and Bane could totally take.

Bane puffed out his chest and made a move to go at the woman. Weston shook his head, grabbing his friend. "Smells like a stall tactic."

Bane exhaled loudly and then stepped back. "Agreed. We should go."

The shaved head chick looked worried. "What about your friends? We have some of them held captive."

He took Paisley's hand and led her through the opening in the wall rather than the door, since the door was now blocked by carnage. Bane followed close behind. Neither said a word more to the woman or about what she claimed to be fact. They headed toward the front of the club, the back now piled high with dead bodies.

If the bitch and her boss were holding operatives, Weston and Bane would get to the bottom of it, but not here and not now. It was time to get while the getting was good and live to fight another day.

Chapter Seven

Paisley stayed close to Weston as he led her through the darkened club. It seemed empty now, but she knew it wasn't. Everyone with any sense was probably hidden. Had she had any sense she'd have never been there to start with.

Closing her eyes briefly, she held tight to Weston's hand as he led her in the direction of the entrance. She thought about Gale and about the vampire's words —they were holding captives. Was Gale one?

She tugged on Weston's hand, getting him to stop.

He looked down at her. "You're not staying here."

"I know, it's just, well, maybe she knows something about my friend," she said, understanding it was dangerous to linger any more than necessary in the place. She'd been lucky to have Weston walk into the room and not whoever was running the show at the club.

She knew that and she was currently looking a gift horse in the mouth. Nothing good would come of it.

Weston's hunky friend bumped into her. "Sorry."

Heat rushed over her as she collided with Weston. When he drew her back to arm's length, she noticed his eyes were dilated. He felt it too.

"Weston?" asked the other man. "You all right there?"

Paisley stared between the men, wondering how it was possible to have two hunks like Weston and his friend occupying the same location. Wasn't that against some sort of universal code? One that kept women from fainting? If not, it should have been. She gulped. They were both very sexy and all male. But Weston won out in her eyes. Not that his buddy was lacking in any way.

It was the makings of an erotic-fantasy sandwich, one to each side of her. The totally hot friend's jeans were barely done up and he was minus a shirt. Like Weston, the man had scars on his body, though his were not as faint as Weston's. A set of the scars lined up so perfectly it looked as if he'd been attacked by a huge animal that had swiped his arm and gotten his torso in the process. And, like Weston, none of the scars took away from how sexy the men were despite the fact that several of the new guy's were much longer.

The man looked at her and quirked a brow before he stole a glance deeper into the club. "Weston, you're taking one for the road? I wasn't aware they offered to-go packages."

Paisley wanted to be offended by the remark, but she glanced at Weston and found whatever she carried inside her kicking into high gear again, making her squirm in place as she watched him there, his muscles bulging, pulling attention to his torso. Man, she loved the guy's abs. She glanced back at the new guy. His were pretty awesome too. Did they work out together? Oh man, she wanted to see that workout session. She could imagine all that hard man muscle just dripping with sweat, the two of them looking like gods with lickable goodness just beading up on them.

"Stop drooling over my friend," snapped Weston, touching her chin and forcing her gaze to his face. His blue gaze was heated and she wondered what was going through the man's mind. From the looks of it he seemed torn between scolding her and pressing her against the wall and fucking her into oblivion.

Hope it's the latter of the two, she thought with a breathy sigh.

"Have you seen him?" she asked, before thinking any better of it. Her mind and body were at war with one another. Too much had happened too fast for her to fully absorb any of it. She knew deep down that she was more than likely in shock. Didn't stop her behavior any, though. "Hard not to drool."

Weston's jaw set and a low growl came from him, making something in her lower body tingle with anticipation. She pushed against him, her gaze on him fully. "Take your shirt off again. I want to drool over you. In fact, I want to lick you."

She sounded a lot like Gale at the moment, and Paisley wasn't sure how she felt about that realization. She almost apologized to Weston for the outburst, but decided it wasn't worth the effort. She did want to drool over him, and her body ached for more than he'd offered her. Much more.

His eyes widened and his friend laughed, the sound deep and sexy. "Man, Weston, your face. This is priceless. Want to tell me why you're not taking her up on the offer to let her lick you? I know you want it. I can smell the desire rolling off you, brother."

"You're brothers?" she asked, glancing between the men. They were both huge and bulky and seemed to be rocking similar close-cut beards, but she didn't see much of a resemblance beyond that.

Weston took her chin in his hand once more, making her look at him. She didn't mind. He was gorgeous. She could have been forced to look at far worse when her body was craving sex. He wasn't a hardship by any means.

"Bane," he said over her head to the man with them. "How do you propose we get out of here? I can smell more of them."

"The rotten smell?" asked Paisley, wondering if it had been the men who attacked them that smelled of death.

"Yep. Hybrid dicks," said the other man. "I swear there must be an assembly line of them nearby. More and more are popping out of the woodwork around here lately. Like roaches."

"And all of them smell like zombies,"

said Weston.

Paisley's eyes widened. "Zombies are real?"

"Shall we exit out the front and make a splash?" asked Weston, grinning.

"That works," said the man—Bane—his hand moving her shoulder. "She's hot. Never thought I'd suggest sharing a woman, but hey, I'm sure they have a price for that here too."

She froze.

Weston roared and the next thing she knew, he was past her and slamming into the man called Bane. Weston pushed Bane over a table and they crashed into a chair, splintering it almost instantly. Snarling, Weston drew his arm back, claws emerging quickly. "She's mine!"

Bane's dark eyes widened as he reached up calmly with both hands, almost in a surrender pose. "You all right there, brother?"

"She is mine!" Weston shouted louder this time.

Bane gasped and then pushed off

Weston, charging a group of men behind them. Paisley stepped back into the shadows, watching as the men once again fought through what she'd had assumed was an unmovable force. She was fast starting to suspect the man claiming to be her mate was actually a superhero. No other way around it.

A jerk at times, but a hero all the same.

She tried her best to stay out of the way, letting Weston and Bane do whatever it was they did. Something yanked hard on the back of Paisley's hair and she yelped as she found herself being dragged backwards by one of the smelly bad guys.

She clawed at his arm to no avail and then kicked her feet, forcing him to slow his pace as she flailed about like a maniac. That got her nowhere fast. She did her best to avoid screaming like one of those women from the movies who seemed to always need to be saved by the big hunky men. She'd grown up on the streets and was hardly a delicate little flower. She wasn't to Weston's level of fighting by any means, but she wasn't a weakling and she wasn't going to be a victim any longer.

The thing dragging her growled and spittle dripped down and onto her arm, turning her stomach. He bent, putting his face dangerously close to hers, his eyes glowing red. He flashed a double row of teeth at her, making her instantly think of a shark. Whatever the thing was, he smelled horrid and was butt ugly. He also wasn't taking her another inch. Not with any ease.

She clawed at his eyes but missed and he grabbed her wrists, slamming them back at the same time he rode her body to the floor, crashing his full weight upon her, knocking the wind from her. Stunned, she lay there a moment, unable to draw in a deep breath.

The monster on her grabbed at the hem of her skirt, and when she wrapped her mind around the fact the thing was pushing her skirt up, trying to get between her legs, she shut off, her body and mind suddenly feeling very relaxed. A strange buzzing seemed to build deep in her at a rate that should have frightened her. It didn't. Deep down she knew it had to be. That whatever was happening to her was a good thing. That it was there to help. Not to hurt her.

The thing on her made progress, his hand skimming her inner thigh. Vaguely, she heard Weston yelling, his voice sounding so much deeper than it already was. Paisley sounded him out, her focus on the monster above her. She let the pressure and buzzing sensation in her build more and did nothing to stop him as he ripped from her, bursting out as if she were an exploding sun. One second the monster was on her and then it was no more.

Gone.

Poof.

Nothing there.

She sat up slowly, the energy seeming to pulse through her, the buzzing loud, the pressure there but not painful in the least. It was almost liberating. It took her a moment to hear over the ringing in her ears, but when she did, she heard Weston yelling for her.

"Let go of me," he shouted. "She needs me!"

"Brother, calm down," said Bane, sounding strained. "You can't touch her right now. Don't you feel it?"

"Let me fucking go!"

"I can't. She's got Fae power rolling off her," said Bane. "If she hit you with it you'll go splat like the other guy too."

Go splat?

Paisley glanced around herself, noting that her body and the area directly around her was clean, free from anything, but beyond that was something her mind couldn't wrap around. Beyond that looked as if a grenade had gone off and only blood splatter remained.

Pink dust.

The thought hit her hard as she realized what she was sitting in the center of—the monster who had been on her. He was now nothing more than pink dust all around her in the hall.

Her mouth opened and she heard someone screaming. It took Paisley a few seconds to realize she was the culprit. Lifting her hands, she stared down at them, the energy she'd felt seeming to lessen, drawing back into her, the buzzing ending, taking the strange calmness with it. She screamed more and scrambled to get to her feet. Twisting, she found Weston being held back at the end of the hall by Bane, who didn't look as though he could hold on much longer.

Paisley continued to scream, keeping her hands up in the air, horrified at what had happened. At what she'd done. She'd never done anything of the sort before.

Weston broke free from Bane and charged her. He snatched hold of her and lifted her off her feet, running with her through the carnage around them. Bane followed close behind. When they burst free from the club, they ran toward a black SUV. Weston set her down and Bane grabbed her hands, lowering them.

"No offense, lady, but I'd rather you not aim those at me," said Bane with a shaky breath.

She blinked up at him, the screaming finally done. "W-what happened?"

"You don't know?" he asked as Weston lifted her into the SUV as if she were a child. He climbed in the backseat with her as Bane ran around to the driver's side.

Weston yanked her against him so hard she couldn't breathe. She had to push on him to get him to loosen his grasp. When he did, he bent his head, his lips instantly finding hers. The kiss was hot and branding, helping her to find her center once more.

As he pulled his head back to look at her, she started to shake again, her hand going to his chest. She shook her head. "I think I just made a man blow up."

"Yep," he said, as if that sort of thing happened to him daily. Maybe it did.

She looked down at her hands, shock still coursing through her veins. "You're not hearing me. I made a man blow up.

Boom. Splat. Poof. Blah. Grr."

When he didn't respond, she met his gaze to find him grinning at her, his blue gaze light and cheery. She shook her head. "Are you not understanding what I'm telling you?"

"Woman, I'm getting every damn word you're saying," he said with a lick of his lower lip. "I, for one, am fucking thrilled you did it."

Her eyes widened. "What?"

"Baby, he was going to do bad things to you," said Weston, his gaze hardening. "And I couldn't get to you fast enough. I'm so happy you turned him into hybrid puree, that all I want to do is roll onto you and spend my seed in you."

Bane cleared his throat from the front seat as he drove. "If we could refrain, that would be great."

Weston laughed. "Did you see her, Bane? She was amazing."

"She was something all right," said Bane, his dark gaze on her in the rearview mirror. "This isn't something you knew you could do?"

"No," she whispered. "And I don't ever want to do it again."

Weston grumbled. "If you are ever threatened again, you most certainly will puree them. Do you understand me? You're my mate, and if I say you explode someone to protect yourself, you better damn well obey."

"Obey?" she asked, the word tasting sour.

Weston pursed his lips. "Not obey. Obey was a poor choice of wording."

"Huh," said Bane from the front seat. "I was sort of stuck on the whole use of the word mate."

Weston rubbed the back of his neck. "Yeah, about that."

"Is anyone else super tired?" asked Paisley, feeling as if the weight of the last few weeks came crashing down upon her. She sank against Weston's embrace and closed her eyes, bone tired.

Chapter Eight

Weston held Paisley partially on his lap in the back of the SUV as she slept. Bane kept stealing glances at them from the mirror. Weston caught his friend's gaze and held it a second.

"Stop worrying about her. She's no threat to us," said Weston. "And I know what you're thinking. She's not a liability, either."

Bane exhaled loudly. "Actually, I was worried about you, not her. In case you missed it, you verbally laid claim to her to mark her and then you referred to her as your mate."

Weston hadn't missed it. "Yes."

"I thought we were going to the club to blow steam off so we could go searching for this supposed mate of yours," added Bane, making a hard right turn and driving at a speed that would have worried other people. Defensive driving was a skill all the operatives possessed. A learned one. The scientists had ramped up their reflexes so they were pretty much all-around badasses behind the wheel of a car. The men had a lot of skills and an equal number of flaws.

"That had been the plan," replied Weston softly, skimming his thumb over Paisley's cheek, noticing for the first time the hints of olive undertones in her skin. She was a blend of something. Whatever it was left her being the single most beautiful woman he'd ever laid eyes upon. "Plan kind of went out the window when I found her there."

"You're sure she's your mate?" asked Bane as he raised one hand from the wheel to indicate he didn't mean anything bad by asking, but that he had to at least ask.

"Without a doubt," said Weston. "From the second I met her I've been fighting the urge to bite her and claim her fully."

"Heard that was the way of it when mates come into play," said Bane, his voice strained, and from what Weston could see of his reflection in the rearview mirror, the man had a pained expression on his face.

"You'll find your mate," said Weston, wanting to ease his friend's pain. Though, the reality was, no one was assured to have a mate. No one was guaranteed they'd find that person that made them feel whole. Nothing in life was a for sure.

Especially not mates.

Bane didn't respond. He just kept driving, his focus on the road and off the topic of mates. At least verbally. There was no doubt in Weston's mind that Bane was still thinking on it all. Weston hadn't thought of himself as the type of man to want something long term with a woman, especially since he liked to stay on the move. Holding Paisley in his arms changed that.

He had a few homes spread around the world that were more than he'd term safe houses or crash pads. They held a little bit of his personality and he tended to spend more time than he should within them.

The government hadn't come knocking in the last few years and he'd started to wonder if maybe they were done trying to track down their Outcasts.

Yeah, right.

"How much longer do we have until we're there?" asked Weston, wondering how long he'd get to simply hold his woman and soak in the sight of her before they reached the safe house.

Bane cleared his throat. "Maybe twenty minutes."

Weston could feel a question coming on from his friend. He was guessing it was one he'd not like with how much beating around the bush Bane was doing to get to it.

"Why was your mate in that type of club?" asked Bane softly as if the volume of the question might lessen its blow.

Weston sighed. "I asked the same thing."

"And the answer was?"

Weston touched her cheek lightly as he spoke. "From what I can gather, she was looking for someone named Gale and she knows Jinx."

Bane glanced back at him. "As in the woman who's mated to Asher Brooks? Colonel with the Immortal Ops?"

"You heard about that too, huh?" asked Weston, not really that surprised. Not much happened within the Ops world that didn't spread like wildfire through varying contacts, eventually reaching the people who needed to know. Sometimes the information came by means that weren't standard—such as Weston's dreams. He wasn't the only Outcast with the gift or curse of foresight. Some were better with it than him. Others didn't have a fucking clue what they were doing.

Bane nodded. "Good for him. But how does your woman know Jinx? She work for her at the brothel?"

Weston's jaw set. "I don't think so. She mentioned something about being there because she needed to feed."

"She's not a vampire," stated Bane clearly. He then tapped the steering wheel lightly. "That vampire chick at the club mentioned the boss had a thing for succubi. Your girl there one?"

"I think so." Weston wasn't sure what Paisley was. All he knew was soon enough she'd be claimed by him and nothing else would matter.

"She's also got Fae in her," said Bane.

"Yeah, hard to miss that one," Weston returned, remembering what it had been like to see Paisley explode a man before his very eyes. "Didn't seem like she was aware of as much though, did it?"

"No. But, Weston, the vampires saw her do it. That boss guy was already wanting her. When he finds out she's possibly more than a mere succubus, he's going to get real about trying to take her. And, Weston, it sounds to me like he's got himself a collection of shiny objects as is."

Weston had to fight the growl wanting to come from him. He didn't want to wake Paisley. "No one is taking her."

"I get it, brother. I do. You know I've got your back, but this might be over our heads." Bane pulled off to the side of the road and turned in the seat to face him. "It might be wise for us to call in some more favors. And we need to find out more about what she said—about having Outcasts held captive."

"It was enough for me to ask you to come out of hiding," said Weston. "I can't endanger anyone else. I already have enough guilt about dragging you into this mess. I'll get Paisley somewhere safe and then I'll go back and see what I can find."

"We're your brothers, bear-face, it's what we do," said Bane with a smirk.

Weston shook his head. "No. I won't bring them into this. I might have another option."

"Care to share?" asked Bane. "I'm all ears."

"Open to working with some PSI-Operatives?"

Bane touched the seat next to him. "Can we trust them?"

"Probably."

"How reassuring."

Weston shrugged. "It's all I got. And Casey trusts them."

"Then I'll trust them too. When we get to the house I'll make some calls and see what I can do on my end," said Bane. "In the meantime, keep an eye on her and I'll arrange for transportation out of Seattle."

"Thanks, brother." Weston's body tightened and the stirrings of need rushed through him. His beast still wasn't sated. It hadn't had sex and it hadn't been permitted to roam free. As the itch to change hit him hard, he gasped, sitting upright in the seat, putting his hands up, fearful they'd shift without him meaning to and cut Paisley as she slept.

Bane groaned. "You didn't sleep with

her, did you?"

"No."

Bane leveled a hard gaze on him. "And why not? She was in a whorehouse."

Weston wanted to be angry but was too nervous about fully shifting forms to let himself go there. Besides, Bane did sort of have a point. "I wanted to do the honorable thing."

"Well, the honorable way is going to get you chained in the changing room of the safe house for the night," muttered Bane, pulling back onto the road and spewing a line of obscenities as he did.

Weston knew he was right. He'd need to be chained for the night to make sure he didn't hurt Paisley. Come morning he'd do a full shift, do a run and then jack off. He wasn't in the state of mind to try any of the remedies now. He'd only end up hurting someone, and it wasn't smart to send him, fully shifted, out at nighttime. Who the hell knew what he'd get up to?

"When we get there, chain me and watch over her, okay?"

Bane nodded. "You're still an asshole."

Weston shrugged. "Yep."

"It's all I got."

"Hey, Bane," said Weston, lifting his hand as claws began to emerge from his fingertips. He tried to calm himself to make them go back in, but it didn't work. He'd put too long between shifts and sex. Way too long. "Get the chains as soon as we pull in."

Bane glanced back at him. "Shit. Okay."

Chapter Nine

"Is she dead?"

Paisley stirred awake to the sound of a rather loud male voice close to her head. She blinked up and did a double take, sure she was dreaming. What else could possibly explain the crazed-looking older man bent over her, staring at her from behind flight goggles while wearing a snorkel breathing tube, currently pushed up onto his nose? Gray hair stuck out all over his head and she had to wonder if the man had ever brushed it, let alone washed it.

She moved away from him slightly,

trying to get her bearings. Last check she'd been in an SUV with Weston and Bane, headed somewhere safe. Was this the safe place?

She eyed the small man more as he smiled widely at her.

"Oh, you are alive," he said, standing back, giving her a full view of him. He had on oversized swim trunks that hung past his knees, a t-shirt with an odd slogan on it that read "Have Stake Will Use," and the best part was he was in orange arm floats like one would see on a small child in a pool. They were stretched over his rather hairy, chubby arms. There was no way they would do anything in the way of holding him up in water.

"Gus, you were right," said the small man. "You said she was alive. I thought she was dead and would start stinking up the place. Corpses are the worst. I mean, the smell of them doesn't just wash out of things. It lingers. Like the smell of fish after a few days of sitting in the sun."

"Excuse me, but who are you and

where am I?" she asked, noticing another man in the room for the first time. This one was markedly taller than the other, but very, very skinny. He didn't meet her gaze.

He had on a tiny swimsuit that she quickly realized were not men's bottoms but rather women's. They barely covered him. If he turned around she was fairly sure she'd get a peek at his exposed butt cheeks. Something that made her lip curl. He didn't have on a shirt like the other. But he did have flippers on his feet and full snorkel gear on his head.

"Who are you?" asked the small, hairy man.

"I asked you first," she pressed, looking them over, wondering if maybe they were escaped mental patients.

"You did ask first," said the hairy man. "I'm Bill. That's Gus. We're your protectors. I'm sort of famous around this group. See, I'm known as Wild Bill, the great mechanical elephant tamer. Gus here doesn't really speak much out loud."

He tapped his head. "I hear him in here. He's a genius. He knows things other people don't. He knew you'd need our help. That we all had to come to Seattle for you. He was right. So, yeah, we're here to help save you."

"I feel better already," she said, trying not to laugh at the sight of the two of them. "Is Weston here?"

Bill nodded. "He's busy right now, but he'll be back around in the morning. We're not to bother him right now. Bane said he'll probably eat us for sure if we do."

"Eat you?" she asked, sitting up slowly. There was a change of clothes set out for her on the end of the bed. A pair of sweatpants and a t-shirt along with a thong. Interesting choice to pair with sweatpants.

"Bane asked us to look in on you while he ran to get some food," Bill said, smiling wide. "We ate all that he had here."

Gus nodded behind him, looking toward the wall.

"Gus says it was yummy," Bill added.

Gus hadn't said a word.

Paisley didn't comment, but rather watched the men, feeling her mood lighten around them greatly. Whoever they were, they were amusing and seemed harmless enough.

"I gave you our names, what is yours? Bane calls you *that woman*. Bet that isn't really your name, is it? Though, I once knew a woman who was named Boy. That was weird. Met her while I was in Vietnam. She was nice. Pretty. Banged her a few times. She wanted marriage. I had to explain I'm a playboy and have to keep myself available for the ladies. She understood."

Paisley had to fight to hide her laughter. "Yes, you're very suave. I can see how the women would want to snag you for their own."

He adjusted the t-shirt, pride on his face. "I know, right? I'm not hung like these shifter guys, though. I saw your man's dick. It was huge. I think they got a better deal out of their government testing.

I might go in and ask for the scientist to make mine bigger too. Have you seen theirs? Horses, I tell you. Horses."

Gus turned in a circle.

"Gus says mine is fine. He's just being nice," said Bill, glancing at Gus. "You wanna see, *that woman*?"

It took her a moment to follow. When she realized he was offering to show her his package, she yelped, putting a hand up. "No. I'm good. We'll take Gus's, um, word for it."

Gus still hadn't said a peep. She wasn't sure he even could talk.

Bill's smile faded. "No one lets me free Willy."

"Probably for the best," said Paisley. "I wouldn't want to be too taken with you to go on with my day, and it sounds to me like you don't need yet another woman trying to get you to marry her."

Bill rubbed his jawline and then nodded to her. "You're smart and pretty. Best I not show you mine. Yogi would be upset if I stole you from him. So, wanna swim? We're going in."

"Yogi?" she asked.

"Weston."

She couldn't stop a small laugh from escaping. "I'd like to shower and change my clothes."

Bill motioned to her with a careless wave. "Nah, just jump in the pool in your clothes. It will get you good and cleaned up. We brought you a swim ring. We didn't know if you could swim. That, and I wasn't sure if you were dead or not. I'm pretty sure dead people float, but I brought the ring just in case you sank."

Placing her hand over her mouth, she tried to keep from laughing but failed, and masked it as a cough. "Thank you."

Gus tipped his head, looking almost at her.

Bill grunted. "He's right. We don't know your name yet."

"Paisley," she said with a gentle smile. The need to be kind to them was great.

Bill quirked a brow. "Got a sister named Plaid?"

She snorted. "No."

"That's a damn shame," said Bill, thumbing backwards. "We got a buddy who is Scottish and he'd probably really like a woman named Plaid. He's always wearing that skirt thing and it's plaid."

Gus tipped his head to one side and Bill snorted then spoke. "I know it's called a kilt; you don't have to shout."

"Should I find out I have a sister named Plaid, I'll be sure to keep him in mind for her," said Paisley, her heart warming to the men. There was an innocence about them that made her want to protect them.

"Thanks," said Bill, touching Gus's arm lightly. "We can tell Striker that we may have found him a woman should a secret twin pop up." Bill shook his head. "No, I don't know the odds of that."

He paused, seeming to hear Gus when no words were spoken at all. That, or he was just making things up as he went.

"Oh, those are not great odds," said Bill. He looked to her. "Ready to swim?"

"Can I shower instead, and then maybe

come out and join you both and watch you swim?" she asked, her voice soft.

Bill appeared upset but nodded all the same. "Okay, bathroom is that way. Oh, don't go to the basement. Bane will get mad and Weston might eat you. He's such a grumpy bear that Bane had to chain him up down there."

Gasping, Paisley stood. "Weston is chained in the basement?"

Gus made inaudible noises through the snorkel tube and spun around faster and faster, waving his arms about. She wasn't sure if he needed medical attention or if he was just upset.

Bill grabbed his hand and then patted, calming the other man instantly. "She knows we didn't chain him to be mean. She's smart. Didn't you hear her figure out how she'd be so attracted to me that if I freed Willy, she'd be clingy? That is one smart woman there, even with being named after a pattern found mostly on coaches and men's ties."

Paisley gave in to laughter and both

men looked at her. She laughed so hard she hiccupped.

Bill grinned. "See? All better. She's not mad at us. She knows Weston is a bear-shifter and I'm guessing she knows he's dangerous to be around. That is why he made Bane chain him. He didn't want to hurt her."

Gus headed for the door and Bill hurried after him. "But we ate all the goldfish crackers. Bane said there aren't any more." He grunted. "Were-gorillas are total liars. Let's go raid his hidden stash."

They stalled in their progress near the door. Bill turned to her. "They don't think I know where they hid my drugs. I have some good shit. Need anything?"

She blinked. "Uh, I'm good. Thank you."

"Nothing beats a joint and junk food, Paisley. Nothing at all."

With that, they left the room, leaving her standing there, totally at a loss for words as to what she'd just been part of. Once she was sure they were gone, she tiptoed from the room in search of the basement.

Chapter Ten

Testosterone charged the air the deeper she descended into the basement of the expansive home. In the movies, the safe houses people went to always seemed sparse and barely useable. This one was huge and decorated with high-end furnishings. A mansion, especially compared to where she grew up.

She'd finally managed to find the door to the basement, all the while wondering if she'd run into Bane. From the way Bill had gone on about Bane, he wouldn't have permitted Paisley to seek out Weston, and that simply wasn't an option.

The pull she'd felt to the man was still there, more so than ever, and she had to check on him. She had to be sure he was well. He'd protected her and had even killed for her. The least she could do was assure he was okay and as comfortable as he could possibly be.

As the pads of her feet connected with the cool concrete floor of the basement, she heard the rattling of chains. The sound intensified the deeper she went into the basement. Doors lined the long hallway. She peeked in one darkened room and gasped when she realized it was a padded cell. When she stepped out and looked up and down the long corridor, she got the distinct impression the basement was more like a self-contained prison than what anyone else would use the area for.

Weston had made Bane chain him down here?

But why?

She'd seen the man at least partially shift forms already, and she'd not run away screaming from him. Why hide from her now?

"Weston?" she asked softly, unsure if he would be the only person she'd find chained in the area.

A low growl greeted her whisper and she followed the sound to the very end of the hallway. The door on the left side was closed and she stood on her tiptoes to try to see through the small window access located high up on it. Her stomach tightened at the sight of Weston in the dimly lit room, his wrists and ankles bound as he laid there naked on the cold, hard floor.

Gasping, she pushed the pin in the door handle up and released the door, swinging it open wide. Weston's head shot up and he looked at her from extremely dark eyes—not his blue ones.

Her breath caught at the feral expression on his face.

Where was the man who had saved her?

"G-Go!" he shouted through clenched teeth.

Shaking her head, Paisley held her ground, her hand on the doorframe. "Why are you down here?"

He turned his face from her and huddled against the back corner. It was evident he didn't want her seeing him this way and that tore at her gut. The man had saved her life, risking his own in the process. Seeing him struggle for control hurt her deep within. Unable to stop herself, she covered the distance between them, coming just shy of touching him.

"Weston, please look at me," she pleaded.

He stiffened and then growled loudly. "Go!"

"No."

That did it. He turned and faced her, tipping his head in a move more animal-like than human. He ran his tongue over his teeth and she noticed then they were longer than normal. Another sign he was losing control. She reached out, half-expecting him to push her hand away with his current behavior. He didn't. He allowed her to touch his scruffy jaw.

"I want to help you," she said, going to her knees, ignoring just how naked the man was. This wasn't a time for her to think upon anything but his well-being. The side of herself that hungered for sex was there, pushing to be free, but she held tight to it, even going so far as to hold her breath a second, as if that might help to keep it at bay.

It didn't.

She had to break her touch with Weston, fearful she'd push him too far. He caught her wrist gently in his large hand, and his chains rattled more. He inhaled deeply, drawing her closer to his huddled form. Her hunger rose as she caught the manly smell of him.

"Berries and cream," he said, his voice still deeper than normal.

Confused, she merely stared at him, letting him hold her closer as her gaze slowly eased over his form. The man was amazing to behold. It was hard to think about anything other than licking his skin when he was close to her. Paisley gave in and did just that. She licked his upper chest and he jerked her hard against his body, exposing his erection to her.

It was long, thick and hard, bobbing there between them, so close for the taking. She used her free hand to take hold of his shaft as best she could, her fingers not fitting all the way around his girth.

Weston roared, the sound loud and partially deafening, but she didn't scream or even feel fear. She felt excitement race through her. She understood the cry, knew that it meant primal need, and she was willing to give him whatever he needed.

Including her virginity.

Her mind spun with all the times she'd gone out of her way to avoid handing it over to just any man. But Weston wasn't any man. He was the man she'd been holding onto it for.

My mate.

She stroked him more and he shook

his head. "Paisley, no. Go. I could hurt you. Fuck. I *will* hurt you."

She pushed on his shoulder hard enough to catch him off balance and he nearly toppled over. Wasting no time, she scrambled onto his lap, her lips going directly to his. His hands found her hips and he eased up her skirt, his tongue racing around hers as they each moaned. She ground her hips on him, his cock trapped against her low stomach, there, so close for the taking.

Weston growled in her mouth and then she heard ripping as he tugged at her panties. Cool air met her backside and she understood then he'd just torn off the barrier between them. Her hunger pounded at her from within, demanding more, demanding to be fully sated—finally.

She tugged her t-shirt over her head and threw it to the other side of the cell. Weston's clawed fingers found her bra and he shredded it, never once cutting her skin. The man may have feared being totally out of control, but his actions said he had it all well in hand.

She broke the kiss and met his gaze, her hand on his cock as she eased up, lining him up with her wet entrance. "I want you."

He shook his head. "You're not ready, baby."

She slid down onto him, pain lancing through her as the last bit of resistance she had broke away. Weston slammed his chained arms back, the sound loud as the chains rattled more and the room seemed to shake. He let out a cry that was purely animal as she sank deeper onto his shaft, feeling as though she might split in half. She didn't care. The extreme fullness was what her body craved. She wanted him deep in her, wanted to be one fully with him.

After several long agonizing minutes she was finally on him. Paisley glanced down at herself, surprised all of him had managed to fit in her. She then touched his face, forcing him to look at her.

"Touch me," she said, moving slowly on

him, riding him at that pace until her body grew more accustomed to having something the size of him in it. Weston moved his jaw around and the cords in his neck popped out, signaling he was straining. She increased her movements, riding him faster and harder.

He grabbed her hips, the chains smacking her thighs as he did, the pain somehow managing to bring with it pleasure and excitement. Her hunger doubled and she arched her back, letting him control the thrusts. Letting him be the leader in their erotic dance. He pulled her down onto him with hard yanks, each time making her wonder if he'd break right through her. If he did, she'd go up in flames of passion and die happy.

He nuzzled his face against her shoulder and trailed kisses along her shoulder-blade before jerking his head back. "No!"

She kept going, kept moving on him, never wanting the pleasure to end. She'd waited so long to feed her hunger fully that she wasn't about to stop now. It didn't matter if the man fully shifted under her, she wasn't budging.

"Go," he shouted, straining against his chains, trying to buck her free from him.

She caught the sides of his face. "No. Give me this."

He stiffened. "Fighting the need to bite and claim you."

It took her a split second to register what he was telling her. He was going to do it. He was going to mark her as his for good. She didn't need to be told this was a big thing in his world. She understood as much on a baser level, and whatever she carried in her wanted it to come to pass. Wanted to be claimed fully by him.

She exposed her neck to him as she sank deep onto his cock. "Do it."

A gasp from the other side of the cell sounded, a sign they were not alone, but she didn't take her attention from Weston. She couldn't. Her hunger beat at her as if it was about to break free and take control over the situation, and she doubted very much if it would play nice or worry about anyone getting hurt.

"Mine!" Weston roared and then grabbed her hips, holding her on him as pleasure assailed her, his mouth moving to her shoulder. There was pinching, then pain, followed by her entire body tightening before exploding in bliss. She cried out, moving on him more, his mouth still locked onto her shoulder. Paisley dug at his upper arms as her pussy convulsed around his cock, taking all of the seed he was spilling into her. Finally, her hunger felt as if it had been fully fed.

She paused as she realized she'd drawn blood on him. The strangest urge to lean forward, say mine and lap up the blood hit her hard and she did just that. The minute her tongue made contact with the red drops, energy began to buzz around her. The last time she'd felt anything close to it had been when she'd made a man explode at the club. Fear lanced her and she tried to scramble off Weston.

He released his hold on her shoulder

and locked an arm around her waist before standing, holding her, still in her, demonstrating just how powerful he was. He spun with her, his chains digging into her as he slammed her against the wall, pumping deep in her, controlling their joining.

He pounded into her again and again, drawing another orgasm from her as her energy built, making the air buzz with power. She pushed at him, fearing for him. She didn't want to turn him pink dust. She wanted to love him and be loved by him.

"Weston, no," she managed. "Can't control it."

He pushed harder into her. "Then don't."

"I could hurt you," she said, still pushing on him, but not really wanting him to stop.

He thrust in deep and rubbed his lower half against her, making her cry out in his arms as she came again, her power slamming into him. She screamed, afraid she'd hurt him. When he fucked her almost animal-like against the wall, she understood it didn't affect him the same as others. If anything, the more the energy built, the harder he drove into her and the more her body seemed to soak up all he was offering. She knew she'd be sore when it was over, but she didn't care.

It was worth it.

Every fucking second of it.

Her energy continued to pulse from her and she glanced lazily over Weston's shoulder as he pounded into her. Bane stood in the doorway to the cell, his mouth agape, his eyes wide. She wasn't shocked to see him. Not with the sexual energy riding the air. It was probably like a beacon to shifters.

Paisley offered a warm smile in his direction, feeling wanton and then focused fully on her man, biting at Weston's ear, loving the feel of him in her. Loving being held by him and, if she admitted it to herself, starting to love him in the process.

She heard the door to the cell close and

knew Bane had gone. She kissed Weston's cheek. "Harder."

"Yes, wife," he said, slamming into her, his chains making the walls shake as he did.

Chapter Eleven

Weston stirred, his bear waking him, demanding he be alert and on guard. His attention went straight to Paisley. She was asleep against him, their naked bodies against one another as they spooned on the floor. Clean clothes were set just inside the doorway along with the keys to the chains. Bane had apparently been back at some point, though Weston had never heard him. He'd been too preoccupied with claiming his mate and then making love to her thirteen times.

He shook his head slightly. Sure, he was an alpha male shifter with great stamina, but even in shifter community thirteen times in one night was quite an accomplishment. Grinning like a fool, he stared at his wife, knowing it was her doing. There was no doubt in his mind she was at least part succubus. Her hunger for sex mirrored his own, and he knew her power had been what had ridden the air between them, keeping him going long after his body was spent. Hell, he'd expended so much energy making love to his woman that he didn't feel the need to shift. His bear was quiet, almost hibernation-like kind of silent.

He laughed softly. The damn bear was too sated to much beyond wake him.

His laughter faded as he looked around the cell, realizing how and where he'd claimed his woman. He wasn't proud of it, of his lack of control, of her having to take control of the situation, but he had to admit to being damn happy she was officially his now.

My mate.
My wife.

A smile tugged his lips. He ran a hand through her hair, careful not to let the chains still hooked to his wrists hit her. She stirred slightly, looking up at him through sleepy lids.

"Mmm, hello," she said, her voice making his cock harden.

She nudged his cock with her backside. "Wow, does he ever sleep?"

"Not with you near me and naked, no," said Weston honestly. He'd never get enough of her. Ever. He motioned to the clothing and the keys. "How about we get me unchained and then I take you upstairs and make love to you properly?"

"I'm starving," she said. "Are you hungry?"

He kissed her neck and his cock stirred to life. "I am. I have a small problem, though. I don't think I can walk just this second."

She arched forward somewhat and reached between them, taking his cock in her hand and lining it up with her pussy from behind. "Nothing small about it. We could handle this problem here and now, and then get you unchained." She pressed back and onto his cock head.

Weston took hold of her hips and dragged her onto his cock fully, moving his hips, fucking her while they lay spooned together. It wasn't a position that had appealed to him prior to Paisley. Now he loved it. He drove deeper into her, holding her hips against him, wanting to pound right through her.

She moaned and twisted, their lips locking. Damn if the woman didn't make him feel like all he wanted to do in life was hold her like this, buried deep in her, loving her until his dying breath.

As it should be, he thought.

She broke the kiss and stilled in his arms. "As what should be?"

Weston gasped as he realized she'd heard his thoughts. He pushed into her deeper and held there, reaching around her hip, dragging his chains over her as he cupped her sex. He rubbed his thumb over her clit and she squirmed on the floor, pushing at his hand, gasping.

"If I come again, I'll die," she said.

He pumped harder into her, rubbing her more as he did. Within seconds, she burst under the weight of his fingers, the walls of her pussy pulling at his cock, drawing his eruption from him. He filled her with hot seed, nuzzling his face against her neck and holding her tight to him. Warmth spread throughout his chest and the strangest feeling of total euphoria came over him.

"Woman, if this isn't love, don't tell me, okay. I don't want to know."

She lay limp on the floor, her body sated. "Pfft, like I'd know what love is."

He didn't comment further, knowing it was too soon to do so, but *he* knew, and he knew damn well he loved her. Sure, it had everything to do with her being his mate and the claiming, but that didn't take away from his love for her. "Mmm, grab those keys for me, baby. Let's get you fed."

"Can we shower then? I'm sticky all

over," she said, smiling back at him.

He waggled his brows. "Sure."

She stilled. "Weston, can you and your friends maybe look into what happened to my best friend Gale?"

"The woman you were looking for at the club?"

She nodded. "No one has seen or heard from her in weeks."

"She didn't clear out with the previous owner?"

"She would have contacted me," said Paisley. "She'd have gotten word to me somehow. We have a special bond. Kind of sister-like."

He nodded in understanding. He shared a brotherly bond with the Ops. "Of course, baby. We'll get with some contacts and see what we can find out."

"Thank you," she said, kissing him gently. "What happens from here?"

He lifted his chained wrist. "We undo me."

She laughed. "I mean with us. We really just met and now we're tied together.

Weird, right?"

Weston kissed the tip of her nose. It wasn't too soon. If anything it seemed to be moving too slow. He wanted her swollen with his babe. He wanted her safely tucked away while he cared for her and they started their life. There would be no more running for him. Not now. He'd staked his claim on her and he wouldn't make her live a life like he'd been living. He had enough properties that it was time he settled in one. His bear side always enjoyed the mountains.

"How do you feel about Tennessee?"

"Never been there," she said, snuggling against him.

"I have a cabin there. It's big. Room for a family," he said, his hand skimming down her to her stomach. "It's a safe place. Trust me."

"Weston, I do trust you. Fully." She sat up slowly. "It's a little early to talk about starting a family, though. We should take time to get to know one another."

"Baby, destiny put us together. We

don't really get a say on the kids' front. And let me remind you of what we've now done fourteen times," he said with a sexy grin.

She smiled. "I know, but, Weston, I need to know about Gale."

"I know you do. Let me get you to Tennessee, to safety, and then we'll all look more into it, okay?" He didn't want to tell her that his gut was pushing him to believe Gale had been taken by the same people who attacked them at the club. That her friend was probably far from Seattle by this point. And that the odds of finding her were slim. He wouldn't dash Paisley's hopes and he'd keep his word. He'd call in favors.

Chapter Twelve

Paisley took a seat on the back deck of the place she'd taken to calling home after three weeks of being with Weston, of being mated. She tucked her legs under her in the chair, sipping her peppermint tea. Her life had been something of a whirlwind and she couldn't have been happier.

"Look what Gus found," said Bill, coming up the back steps. He was dressed as a lumberjack. He'd insisted on the outfit the moment they'd arrived at the cabin in Tennessee. He and Gus had been staying with her and Weston for a few days now, calling it a vacation. Weston had been opposed to having them come, but had finally given in when Paisley admitted they made her laugh.

And she needed to laugh.

News had reached her of Gale's whereabouts. Paisley nearly cried just thinking about it. Weston's friends had arrived, each with gazes on the floor, looking grief-filled as they handed him a file. Weston had read it and then looked at her with such sadness that she knew what it said.

Gale was gone. There was no trace of her. She'd not relocated with the rest of the staff from the club to New Orleans. No one had heard from her and the word on the street was that she was dead, though no body had been found. Paisley hadn't wanted to lose hope, but it was hard when everything and everyone kept telling her there was no hope to be had.

Paisley touched her stomach, the tea helping to settle it. Lately, it had been extra touchy. Bill held a container with a butterfly in it as Gus came up the stairs behind him, also dressed like a mountain man.

"She's a beauty, isn't she?" Bill said of the butterfly.

"She is," replied Paisley, sipping her tea again, hoping to chase away the nauseous feeling she'd had since she woke.

"You behaving out here?" asked Weston as he came up from the side, a load of firewood in his arms. The man was born to live in the woods. He seemed so at home and at peace that she found herself loving the area as well. Loving being with him full time and, ultimately, loving him. He was hard not to.

He paused, his arms full of wood. "Woman, you are so fucking sexy that I could seriously eat you up."

Bill waggled his finger at Weston. "No eating her, grumpy bear. It's bad for the baby if you eat its mommy."

Weston's eyes widened and he dropped the armful of wood onto the ground. "W-what?"

Gus turned in a circle and made

motions as if he were trying to catch another butterfly. "Bad for the baby. Really bad for the baby."

Weston looked at her. "We're having a baby?"

She held tight to her tea cup. "I don't think so."

Bill tipped his head, giving her a soft look before sighing. "What do you think all the puking was for this morning?"

She gasped.

Weston leapt up and over the side of the decking without breaking a sweat. He came right for her and bent, his hand going to her stomach. "We need to call James or Green."

She'd met so many men recently that she had a hard time keeping them all straight, but she did remember James from her first night in Tennessee. He'd flown in to check on her, did some minor tests and then left the next day, giving her a clean bill of health before calling later in the week to confirm the succubus and Fae assumptions.

"I'm sure I'm fine, and if we are expecting, I'm sure the baby is fine," she said, touching his cheek. He always seemed so worried about her.

"I love you," he said, stealing a kiss and making her spill some tea onto the arm of the chair.

"I love you too, grumpy bear."

Bill beamed as he held the butterfly. "Who wants to go skinny dipping in the river after breakfast?"

Weston groaned and locked gazes with her. "Let me eat him, please."

"No. He's adorable."

Bill smiled. "Yeah, she's hot for me. Most women are."

Paisley and Weston laughed, holding each other close.

THE END

Dear Reader

Did you enjoy this title and want to know more about Mandy M. Roth, her pen names and all the titles she has available for purchase (over 100)?

About Mandy:

New York Times & *USA TODAY* Bestselling Author Mandy M. Roth is a self-proclaimed Goonie, loves 80s music and movies and wishes leg warmers would come back into fashion. She also thinks the movie The Breakfast Club should be mandatory viewing for...okay, everyone. When she's not dancing around her office to the sounds of the 80s or writing books, she can be found designing book covers for New York publishers, small presses, and indie authors.

Learn More:

To learn more about Mandy and her pen

names, please visit http://
www.mandyroth.com

For latest news about Mandy's newest releases and sales subscribe to her newsletter
http://www.mandyroth.com/newsletter/

To join Mandy's Facebook Reader Group: The Roth Heads, please visit
https://www.facebook.com/groups/MandyRothReaders/

Review this title:

Please let others know if you enjoyed this title. Consider leaving an honest review on the vendor site in which you purchased this title. Reviews help to spread the word and boost overall sales. This means more books in the series you love.

Thank you!

The Raven Books' Complimentary Material
The following material is free of charge. It
will never affect the price of your book.

Act of Mercy (PSI-Ops Series / Immortal Ops) by Mandy M. Roth

Paranormal Security and Intelligence Operative Duke Marlow has a new mission: find, interrogate and eliminate the target—Mercy Deluca. She's more than he bargained for and Intel has it all wrong. She's not the enemy. Far from it. Intel forgot to mention one vital piece of information—she's Duke's mate. And this immortal alpha werewolf doesn't take kindly to her being in danger.

Excerpt from Act of Mercy (PSI-Ops / Immortal Ops) by Mandy M. Roth

Duke Marlow finished typing the last of the reports due into his handler. Corbin handled more than one Paranormal Security and Intelligence Operative (PSI-Op) and Duke already knew he was

Corbin's most trying. He enjoyed getting under the man's skin. Corbin was a panther shifter and everyone knew cats and dogs didn't mix well together. As a full-blooded, born werewolf, Duke tended to get a kick out of giving Corbin as hard a time as possible.

Duke rotated his neck, working out a kink as he sniffed the air, the wolf in him catching the scent of pending rain. He grinned, knowing he'd be running free in it soon enough. Well, as soon as he finished this damn paperwork. He didn't understand the point of it. It wasn't like the organization existed to anyone who asked about it. They were ghosts. Operatives who never were and never would be, at least on paper.

What the fuck did they want with a paper trail then?

The truth of the matter was most of the people within the organization had been there a hell of a long time. Immortality afforded them that luxury. They had some young ones—people under the age of fifty often seemed like pups in his eyes. When you got to his age, most everyone seemed young.

He looked across the main office in PSI headquarters. Rows of desks filled the large bullpen. There was a raised walkway that circled the rounded room. Various doors dotted it. Some were offices. Others interrogation rooms. Some were termed briefing rooms. One was a hallway to restrooms and a kitchen area and the one he disliked visiting most was just past that —the infirmary.

He'd been alive a long time and lost too many people to count that he considered friends, even loved ones. He didn't do well around hospitals or anything of the like. They made him itch. Not as much as planes or anything that flew did.

He fucking hated to fly.

He'd had to fly more times than he'd cared to for the week prior when he'd been called in to help a fellow PSI-Op. Eadan Daly was someone he'd consider a friend. Eadan was young yet, barely thirty, but like Duke he'd stopped aging. Somehow, Eadan, even at his young age within the immortal world, had managed to find love and happiness. He and his mate were together. That was what was important. Not the how or whys of how they'd come to be that way.

Longing still lingered deep within Duke. He wanted what Eadan had. What so many of the I-Ops had—a mate. Wouldn't happen. Not at his age. If his woman had been out there, he'd have found her by now.

He focused on his reports. While they may be done, they still needed to be emailed. Damn, he hated computers. Everyone around him seemed to love them, but he liked putting pen to paper, not fingertips to keyboard. He took a lot of grief at the office about his aversion to certain technologies. He wasn't a luddite, but the others in PSI seemed to enjoy calling him one.

While he would forever look to be in his mid-thirties, he was considerably older.

With that age came the reluctance to accept change with ease. Plus, he was stubborn by nature. And truth of the matter was, most of what he was given technology-wise ended up breaking. In his opinion it was shit.

He'd seen a lot in his life-span. Some good. Some not so good. And some downright horrifying.

An auburn-haired giant poked his head into the room. Striker McCracken was there, grinning a grin that said he was ready to be up to no good. He was Dougal only to his momma, who had been buried over a century. Duke knew his real name because he'd actually met the man's mother way back when. She'd been a sweet woman who managed to be half her son's size, yet still keep him in line nicely.

"You almost done?" asked Striker, traces of the Scottish accent that had once been so thick Duke had a difficult time understanding the man, showing through. "I'm positive the bar at the corner has beers with our names on 'em."

With a groan, Duke emailed off his reports. "I fucking hate this thing," he said, as he tried to get the computer to go to sleep, but it kept instantly waking back up.

"Name one thing you do like."

"Women," returned Duke.

Laughing, Striker came to his recuse. He took the wireless mouse from Duke's grasp. "It's nae gonna shut down with you bumping the mouse. Here. Let me."

Duke slid back in the chair and then stood. "Keep the fucker."

Striker continued to laugh. "You know, if you tried a little harder, you might actually learn to like the thing."

Sliding his long-time friend a hard look, Duke stood silent. No words needed to be spoken. He'd never bond with his damn computer.

.

Printed in Great Britain
by Amazon